Parallel Roads (Lost on Route 66)

By Dennis Higgins

Parallel Roads (Lost on Route 66)

Copyright © 2011, 2012 by Dennis Higgins
All rights reserved. This book or any portion thereof may not be reproduced or used in any manner whatsoever without the express written permission of the publisher except for the use of brief quotations in a book review.

Printed in the United States of America

First Printing, 2011

ISBN-13: 978-1468180947

Publisher: Dennis Higgins; **Create**space (October, 2012)

http://www.timepilgrims.com/

Dennis Higgins

To my beloved wife, Trina who took the journey with me daily.

Parallel Roads (Lost on Route 66)

Chapter 1
It Winds From Chicago...

Grandma disappeared only weeks after giving birth to my dad. She left Chicago via Route 66 on March 22, 1946, but never arrived at Aunt Karen's in Burbank. Today they call it postpartum depression, but back then I'm sure she felt like she had gone insane.

**March
Chicago, Illinois
Present Day**

Not all anniversaries are happy. But few can be as miserable as the day someone drops off the face of the earth.

"Kevin, you know we can't keep putting it off." My mom's voice sounded sad and tired as she looked at me. "We just can't give Grandpa John the care he needs here at home."

"How's Dad taking it?" I asked.

"You know your father and your grandfather as well. It's the anniversary of her disappearance, and I think Grandpa's turn for the worse has a lot to do with that damned date." I could tell she felt stressed because Mom never swore. "Go upstairs and talk to him, Kevin. When Dad gets home, we're driving him to the assisted living home in Northbrook. It's a nice place and will be good for him."

I called my best friend Cheryl for moral support. Living just next door, she arrived in seconds flat. On the way up the stairs to Grandpa's apartment, the same apartment in which he'd lived for close to seventy years, I realized I had to make one last attempt to ask him about my grandma's disappearance all those years ago. Even though Cheryl and I had heard the stories of Grandma Kate and her disappearance for most of our lives, what we actually knew could fill a thimble. There really was more intrigue than fact to the stories. All we had was what Grandpa John had chosen to tell of the incident, Grandma's good-bye note, and a postcard given to us by my Great Aunt Karen announcing her sister's estimated time of arrival.

We knew that Grandma Kate was born Katherine Mary O'Sullivan before marrying Grandpa. They met in the summer of 1939 at a family get-together of a mutual friend in Evanston, Illinois. Grandpa once said that it was love at first sight, but Aunt Karen had told us quite a different story. She said that Katherine wanted nothing to do with this unkempt gentleman who talked like the Americans and had the most peculiar stare.

Entering his apartment, we found Grandpa sitting in his favorite chair. We could see that he was in a bad way--fighting, argumentative, and struggling for breath. I was ready to jump in and start asking him what he thought had happened to Grandma, why she'd left, if he knew anything, but Cheryl, being Cheryl--and a woman--beat me to the punch, gently asking him instead, "Tell us, Grandpa John, how did you meet Grandma Kate?"

And with that question, his whole demeanor changed. He softened. He closed his eyes. When he opened them again, I knew he wasn't really with us as much as somewhere back then, but he did not speak. The thoughts and memories he was experiencing lived only in the dark recesses of his mind. We knew at that moment he was there again with his precious Kate.

1939
Evanston, Illinois

John noticed her sitting alone at his friend's backyard cookout. He had never seen her before but found he could not look at anything else. He soon realized that his stare was making her uncomfortable. It appeared as though she wasn't sure whether to look away or return his unsettling gaze. John thought she was the most beautiful creature he had ever laid his eyes upon. She had almost black hair, with just a hint of brown that was evident in the summer sun, and the deepest blue eyes. He was ecstatic when his friend Burt and his wife Anne walked him over to be introduced.

Katherine, her name was Katherine. It fit her, he thought. The name was as lovely as she was.

"Lovely to make your acquaintance," said Katherine, quickly looking away once again.

John noticed she had the distinctive accent of his ancestors who spoke of their Irish homeland. He didn't know what to do or say; he just knew he had to get to know this creature of loveliness. They were standing near the food table, so looking around, he grasped at the first thing to come to his mind.

"Kate . . . do you mind if I call you Kate?" he asked.

"Indeed I do. Me name is Katherine."

"Good, we're on a first name basis already! Well, then, Kate, may I offer you some fruit?"

"Begging your pardon," she answered, looking surprised.

"Fruit . . . may I offer you some of this fine fruit?" he asked again.

Now she finally looked him squarely in the eyes. "We just met, and the only thing you can offer a lady is fruit?"

But it was at that very moment when her heart softened as she saw the quirkiest look come across his face--half embarrassed, half hopeful.

"Mr. Callahan . . ." She was about to say that a lady is quite capable of obtaining fruit onto her own plate, but instead she found herself saying, "I would love some fruit, good sir. But Mr. Callahan . . ."

"John," he interrupted.

Ignoring him, she began again, "Mr. Callahan . . ."

"John." he interrupted again.

"Oh all right, *John*. Please don't be presuming that just because a lady accepts fruit from a total stranger that she is in any way obliged to him."

"Good pineapple, ain't it?" he asked.

"Yes, quite good, but I think you are changing the subject." she replied.

"What was the subject again?"

"The subject was about you presuming . . ."

He cut her off. "Oh yes, I remember, you were about to say you would accompany me to dinner and a picture show next weekend."

"I was?"

"Oh, yes."

"All because of fruit?" she asked.

"Well, you have tried the strawberries, haven't you?"

"I have."

"And?" John's eyes sparkled.

"Yes, they are also quite good."

"Well, it's settled then," he said.

"Which picture show?" she asked, giving up.

"Well," he answered, "I hear that L. Frank Baum story is quite a hoot. Or how about that Civil War picture?"

This just about summed up the difference between John and Katherine. He was a *Wizard of Oz* sort of guy, whereas she was *Gone with the Wind*. They found love that summer, and by spring of the following year, on May 18, 1940, they were married at Saint Clement Catholic Church on Deming Place in Chicago.

1940–41
Albany Park
Chicago, Illinois

John's parents helped them find a nice affordable apartment in Albany Park. A supervisor of John's dad by the name of Irvine Jacobson told him about the apartment building his parents owned. The upper floor was for rent, as the last tenants had recently moved out due to a job transfer. The Jacobsons were nice enough to allow them to break the lease, but this left them in a bind. So having new tenants would help them out as well as the newlyweds. To be Irish in Albany Park was a bit unusual in this Jewish Chicago neighborhood, but they couldn't ask for better landlords than the Jacobsons. As it turned out, Kate and John were just ahead of the neighborhood integration that would occur after men returned from the war in just a few years.

They busied themselves painting the walls and refinishing the floors. John surprised Kate with a used Victrola and classic Irish music on 78 records. Something about this music saddened her, so she later found some jazz and big band records to play instead. They also listened to the large RCA radio that stood in their front room.

One night John grabbed Kate by the hand and started dancing with her. "John, what will the neighbors think?" she asked. "We haven't proper draperies yet."

"They'll think we are two crazy Gentile kids who are madly in love," John answered.

"Crazy is right," Kate said smiling.

"Kate, soon I'll be able to afford that honeymoon I promised you."

"Oh? I don't remember you promising me a honeymoon," she answered. "And just where will ye be taking me?"

"Well, let's see now . . . Bermuda, Hawaii, Tahiti? How about back to Ireland?"

"No sir, not interested. What else might you offer?" she asked.

He dipped her gracefully. "Well, we could do a domestic honeymoon like Niagara Falls or the Grand Canyon. I've always wanted to see the Grand Canyon, Kate."

"How about Saturn, John? We could fly among the stars and ride on the rings of Saturn."

"All right, my doll face, I will take you to Saturn. But right now, Mrs. Callahan, I would like to take you to our bedroom."

"I graciously accept, Mr. Callahan," she said softly.

* * * * *

By July, Kate had discovered she was with child. John was ecstatic and Kate thought that life just couldn't get any better. Then one night as they relaxed in front of the radio, they heard the devastating news. A Japanese fleet had attacked the naval base at Pearl Harbor. America was at war. Although Kate thought it was awful and it angered her, she didn't believe it would affect her and John and their life together. But then Hitler continued to spread his evils across Europe, leaving the whole nation in a patriotic frenzy. All of John's friends were enlisting, and he knew he had to do his duty as well. Kate was upset when he revealed his plans, but she also knew it was what the men had to do.

One morning, Kate woke up to intense pain. "John, help, something is terribly wrong!" she cried.

"Kate, what is it, darling?" He asked, waking up quickly.

"Call Doctor Butler," she said between grimaces. "John, there's something the matter with the baby. I just know it!"

Doctor Butler and a nurse arrived at the apartment, and Kate's greatest fear was realized. She had lost the baby just three weeks before John's departure.

The days that followed were terribly difficult and Kate struggled to climb out of her intense sadness. But for John's sake and her own sanity, she did her best to overcome her sorrow and was able to feign moments of normalcy once again.

She was even able to stand there with her husband at the Chicago Municipal Airport to say her last good-bye before his overseas deployment.

"Kate, I'm gonna miss you like crazy," John said as he held her tight. "I wish I wasn't going just yet."

Kate stayed strong for John's sake. She had to let him know that it was all right. "John, go now and do what you have to do. You will make me proud. I will write you as often as I can."

"I'll write you, too," he said. "Are you sure you will be all right?"

"I'll be fine, now stop freighting about me," she answered. "I'll be startin' the new job at the factory soon, and I have your mum and dad here and also the Jacobsons to take care of me. You just do your time and come back safely."

"I will."

"No, promise me, John. Promise me you won't take undue chances. Promise me you will come home to me."

"I promise, darling," he said. "I'll learn to duck."

Kate kissed him and held him tightly until it was time to watch him walk away.

November
Present Day

I guess Cheryl was a private investigator years before she officially got her license. The holidays were a slow time in her detective field, so she resurrected her hobby, the digging and probing operations regarding Grandma Kate. She decided to interview Grandma's former employees of Bruning, the factory where she worked for five years cutting blue prints.

Cheryl and I had grown up hearing the stories of Grandma Kate and her disappearance, which naturally held a fascination for me, but it was Cheryl who had become obsessed with it.

Cheryl Bachman was my best friend in the world. She moved in next door to us on Spaulding Avenue near the Kimball Avenue El stop in Chicago when we were seven. Even back then Cheryl was always trying to dig and uncover tidbits of information.

My full name is Kevin Michael Callahan. Like my father before me and his father before him, I am a railroad man. However, unlike them, who used sweat and muscle all the working days of their lives, my work is filled with the complicated electronics of new train controls.

Cheryl and I were an unlikely pair growing up. For one, she was a girl. She didn't play baseball or trucks or superheroes. But, oh, the adventures she took me on playing spies or secret agents. Another big difference was that Cheryl's roots were German and Jewish, while my family originated from Dublin City in Ireland. We went to different schools as well. Cheryl was a public school kid, while I attended Catholic school. She was a straight A student whereas I, well . . . wasn't. While I went to Mass, she attended Sunday morning Hebrew school. We never got into the name calling that other kids did. I didn't mind being called a "cat licker," "fish eater," or "mackerel snapper," while "heb," "JAP" and "Jewlet" just rolled off her back. Sometimes we heard "Jew lover" and "Meshugeneh" by our own people. I once punched a kid in the nose for telling her she was going to hell because she didn't believe in Jesus. Like I said, she was my best friend.

Cheryl was able to obtain company records from Bruning of Katherine M. Callahan, which were of little use. All they stated was that she made eighty-five cents an hour when she started and $1.26 in her last year. She never missed a day's work until her maternity leave and only had one warning in her permanent record. Apparently, Grandma had a temper and found herself in an altercation with another female worker. No reason was given. It wasn't until Cheryl found and interviewed past co-workers that we were able to fish out the entire story. Most helpful was Mrs. Lidia Majewski, who was closest to Grandma at that time.

"Oh, I remember that day," started Mrs. Majewski with a slight Polish accent. "The woman's name was Franklin . . . June, I believe. Yes, June Franklin. She was a nasty one, she was. She was always picking a fight with Katherine, mocking her accent, calling her a dirty 'Mc.' I have to tell you, dear Katherine was the cleanest woman I'd ever known. She was also very patient with this June person. She treated her with kindness and even took the blame for her when she was on probation, just so she wouldn't lose her job. But this Franklin woman didn't return the kindness. It was just too much when she told Katherine in regards to losing her baby that God must have had a reason to not want another Irish mouth to feed, or something along that line. Katherine just lost her wits about her. The next thing we knew, she had June by the hair and had dragged her all the way down to the factory floor. She was yelling at the woman to never talk about her baby or her personal life again. The woman was screaming for her to stop, and one of the men had to pull Katherine off her.

"Holy cow," I said. "I had no idea."

Well, Franklin reported it, and Katherine was put on probation and docked three hours pay. I remember it was a Friday, and Katherine was so upset that I talked her into taking the El downtown to Harding's Restaurant, where I bought her a nice dinner. I tried to talk her into going to the amusement park, Riverview, for a few laughs, but she told me she was just too tired. I did however manage to get her on the Irving Park streetcar to the ice cream parlor, The Buffalo for a small sundae before going home. After the war ended, this June person just disappeared. We never heard from her again."

Cheryl had no luck tracking down June Franklin, since it was such a common name. Besides, none of this had anything to do with Grandma's disappearance. But for Cheryl, it was just another piece of the whole picture, as she had put it.

The other pieces were the letters that Grandpa had brought back from the war with him. He saved every one she had written. They were full of love and gave him a sense of her everyday life in Chicago. There were no real useful details. Just everyday tidbits to make him feel like she was holding up the fort, waiting for his return. They painted a picture of a happy woman, although that could have been a facade for his sake. Grandpa must have cherished these. We never knew where he kept them, but he had sometimes pulled them out for us to read over the years, a few at a time. Grandpa John must have been a different man from the man we knew. My grandmother's disappearance changed him somehow. He never fully recovered from it, and now, in the nursing home, he never would. We only had tidbits of his memories of the last days leading up to his precious Kate's disappearance from his and everyone else's world.

1945
Chicago

John Callahan was sent home on the first wave after the May 8, 1945, V-E Day. Kate was as excited as a kid at Christmas, pacing for what seemed like hours. His mother and father were with her at the apartment, awaiting his arrival. When the door flew open, Kate and John flew into each other's arms, their bodies becoming one person, one soul. The joy was so intense it hung in the air; it covered the entire city. Later, they dined on his mother's wonderful pot roast and mashed potatoes. They popped the cork on a bottle of champagne that Kate had been saving ever since receiving it from the Jacobsons, a thoughtful gift the first Christmas after John was deployed.

That night as they lay down to bed, they held each other for the longest time, embracing the quiet moment. Finally, Kate broke the silence as John lit a cigarette. "John, are you as happy as I am now that you're home?"

"More so," he answered.

"Won't ye be missing all those other women?" she asked.

"What other women?"

"The ones I read about in *Vanity Fair*," she replied.

"What fair?"

Ignoring him, she went on. "The article said the loneliness was so great for our boys overseas that even the good ones took girls for themselves. It said it was not uncommon for them to be taking up with French girls."

"I suppose it happened." He turned to snub out his cigarette.

"Well?" she asked.

"Well, what?" John now turned to look at her.

"Do you miss your French girl?"

"There was no French girl," he answered.

"Come on, John! In the whole of France, you mean to tell me there are no French girls?"

"You know what I mean," he said. "Although come to think of it, there was one girl."

"I knew it," Kate said with hurt in her voice. She turned away. "Did you offer her fruit?"

"Nope, a Hershey Bar," John voice became solemn. "She was about six and lost. I brought her to my sergeant. I think one of the WACs later took her to the convent. Poor kid! I have a feeling she lost her parents."

Kate turned back around to look at him. "Was it hell, John?"

"War always is, you know," he said. "But Hitler has been stopped, and now I'm back here with you." They hugged and turned off the light.

"Kate?"

"Yes, love."

"Can you talk with a French accent?"

After she socked him in the arm, they made love for the first time in four years.

They must have continued holding each other the entire night, as John found her still cradled in his arms when he awoke the next morning. He lay there for a while, just enjoying the moment. Kate stirred as if she sensed her husband's thoughts.

"Good morning, hon," John said, looking happy.

"Good morning," Kate answered groggily. "Is everything all right?"

"Sure," he answered. "I was thinking, let's hit the town tonight. Dinner out, and then how about I take you dancing? It will be like old times."

"The Aragon Ballroom?" she asked. "That would be lovely, John, but aren't you tired?"

"Nope," he answered. "I feel like I could dance the night away. Besides, I need to have a beautiful woman on my arm instead of that old rifle."

They took John's old 36 Buick Special. This eggplant-colored automobile had been his pride and joy when they met, although it was now a bit rundown.

Kate gasped when they pulled up in front of Alice Baum's on Sheridan Road. "John, how can we afford this?" she asked.

"Tonight is a present from my folks," he answered. "Not to worry, sweet princess."

* * * * *

Alice Baum's Dining Room was a well-known eating parlor. Before stepping into the lobby, Kate glanced across the street at the Saddle and Cycle Club. She remembered hearing about this exclusive club from her aunt's rich friends. She never thought she would be hobnobbing in the Uptown area.

The restaurant was nice, the lobby still decorated from the previous decade. She sat for a moment on the leather davenport and looked at the dessert case. She was hungry. She hoped she was dressed appropriately for such a place. She wore a red rayon dinner dress with cap sleeves and a draped neckline. John looked at her like she was an angel.

The host walked them down the long row of tables and seated them near the room divider. Kate wondered how they got their tablecloths so white. There were other diners who looked up quickly and then went back to their meals and conversations. Kate realized she wasn't as out of place as she felt inside.

The waiter poured water, and John ordered two house rosés. The menu didn't seem to compare with the mansions on either side of the restaurant, just home-style cooked meals such as turkey and pot roast. John ordered a porterhouse steak while Kate had roast chicken.

Putting the napkin on his lap, John asked, "This place is the cat's meow, huh Kate?"

"I would have been happy eating a hotdog at Flukey's, John. I'm just so glad you're home again."

Kate's brogue, although still very present, had faded slightly. Life in the factory the last four years had hardened her. She was no longer a girl from Ireland living in the city. She was now an Irish Chicagoan.

"Kate," John began, "Dad says I can take my time before going back, but my old job is still waiting for me."

"Will you still be happy working downtown at the station?" she asked.

"I've got railroading in my veins. I'll be an engineer soon enough. I still have the Elgin pocket watch Dad gave me before the war."

Kate loathed trains, but she respected John's family who had come to this country and settled in Chicago because of the rails. This was why she had learned to drive an automobile. If she were to ever take a trip, she would not do it by rail.

She smiled at him and patted his hand. "And you'll be a fine railroad engineer at the end of the day," she said, accent in full again. Then her smile faded. "John, you left for Europe at the worst possible time. I almost . . ." She paused, tears welling up in her eyes.

"What is it, Kate?" John said softly. "You almost . . . what?"

"It was just so hard losing the baby and then losing you," she said. "I held the razor blade to my wrist for the longest time. I almost did it, but then I thought of you and how you too had lost our baby and your life here at home. I just couldn't go through with it. You were my lifeline, sweet husband. So I threw the dreaded thing down the toilet and I prayed to St. Brigit for God to forgive my soul."

Kate knew that John wasn't good in situations such as this.

"Promise me that you will *never* do such a thing again," he pleaded. "Promise me, Kate."

"I promise, husband. I promise you as I promised the good Lord that night. Besides," she added as the lilt came back into her voice, "you're not going to be spending our eternity with some other pretty lassie."

Chapter 2
...to LA

December
Chicago
Present Day

"So tell me again, Kevin," Cheryl started. "When did she get pregnant and have your dad?"

"Grandpa said they didn't know it at the time but realized later that she was pregnant already, that very night." I answered.

"Oy vey, that was fast," she said. "You Irish are a fertile bunch, ain't ya?"

Cheryl and I were sitting in her living room looking at Christmas lights across the street. We had just lit the seventh candle on her menorah while she recited the traditional prayer mostly to herself: "Ba-ruch ata, A-do-nai E-lo-hei-nu, me-lech ha-o-lam, she-he-chya-nu ve-ki-ya-ma-nu ve-hi-gi-a-nu las-man-ha-zeh." When Grandpa moved to the assisted living home in Northbrook last spring, my parents had left me in the upstairs part of the house, and Cheryl had moved into the downstairs apartment. Mom and Dad moved to Tennessee to get away from the harsh winters. Dad traveled back to Chicago about twice a month to see Grandpa and to check on me and the house. Technically, my parents still owned the building and Cheryl and I rented from them at a reasonable rate.

"Kev?" she asked. "Remember when we were kids, your mom would take us down to Marshall Field's to look at the window displays and have lunch under the Christmas tree?"

"Ah, yes," I answered. "Good old Field's--I loved the Walnut Room."

"Technically," she said, "it's all still there."

"Come on, Cher," I scolded. "You know better than that." We were still angry that after Macy's purchased Field's, they changed all the stores to the Macy's name. Both Cheryl and I agreed that if we were ever in New York City, we would go to Macy's. We still watched the Macy's Day Parade on

Thanksgiving. But in Chicago, it was Marshall Field's all the way. At present, we had started shopping at Carson Pirie Scott, being true Chicago traditionalists. In fact, last year while at the Kris Kindle Mart--the German Christmas fair held at the Daley Plaza every advent--we sent our friend Jake into Macy's for a box of Frango Mints. We just wouldn't step foot in a Macy's store in the Chicago area. That is, not until they change the name back. So instead, Cheryl and I waited under the big clock that day and ran our fingers across the historic plaque that to this day still reads MARSHALL FIELD AND COMPANY. "Mmmmmm, Frango Mints," Cheryl had said, doing her best Homer Simpson when Jake handed over the box.

Cheryl's blond hair swung as she walked into the kitchen for a cold pop, kissing her hand and touching the Mezuzah left there on the doorpost by the Jacobsons. It had been painted over many times but never removed. Cheryl's education was that of Conservative Judaism at STBZ--whose full name was Congregation Shaare Tikvah B'nai Zion. She now leaned toward the reformed side with a fascination for the Orthodox. She was studying and had become quite learned in the old Hebrew Scriptures, which I called the Old Testament.

Growing up, Cheryl never knew her grandfather, but Bubbe Adi was with us for years. She had distinctive blue numbers tattooed on her arm. During the war at Dachau, we always knew that she had witnessed unspeakable things, so we never spoke of them. I just knew that Cheryl grew up in a loving traditional home. I had to admit that our parents were a little concerned with our friendship at first. But in the end, we just became fixtures in each other's apartments. I didn't realize it at the time, but in retrospect, my mom would always make sure there was something like beef or turkey along with our traditional ham and two sets of china. This way, Cheryl could eat with us at Christmas, Easter, and other family functions. I too would be seated for High Holy Day meals next door at her place. I loved the foods at Rosh Hashanah because they tended to be sweet, like fish with pineapple and honey chicken--and, oh, how I loved Bubbe Adi's challah.

But Cheryl and my favorite time of year was Passover/Easter, especially when they coincided.

Along with holiday meals, we experienced each other's cultures and main events. I attended her Bat Mitzvah when she turned twelve, and she was present at my Confirmation. Both these events meant great parties afterward with cake and presents. During Chanukah, we would spin the dreidel on her kitchen floor, but I had to admit, I never found it to be much fun, especially since Cheryl always won the pot of coins and nuts. Once when we were teenagers, she went to Midnight Mass with me and my family. I laughed to myself when I caught her from the corner of my eye singing Christmas songs at the top of her lungs. We accepted each other as children do, without question. We always knew that God was the same for her as He was for me.

Just then the phone rang.

"Happy holidays," Cheryl answered. "Oh yes, Mrs. Majewski, hi. Really? You're kidding!"

"What?" I asked.

"Shhhhh!" she hushed me. "Yes ma'am," she continued, "that would be great. Yes, it might be very helpful."

"What would?" I asked

"I'll come pick it up. Is tonight okay?"

"Pick what up?"

"Cool," she said. "Okay, bye-bye."

"Kev," she said before the phone even reached the hanger. "Mrs. Majewski found a postcard from your grandmother."

"From where?" I asked.

"I don't know from where yet, dingus, but what interests me is from when. It's postmarked March 23, 1946," she answered.

"Holy crap!" was all I could muster and then I crossed myself.

Lidia Majewski lived in a typical suburban bungalow in Elk Grove Village. Her home was decorated with many pictures of her late husband, kids, and grandkids, with religious articles peppered throughout. A crucifix, an Infant of Prague, and a picture of the late Blessed Pope John Paul II were all prominent. But the epicenter of the room was a large portrait of Our Lady of Częstochowa, also known as the Black Madonna, complete with the two scars on her right cheek. These scars were remnants of when the Hussites tried to steal the portrait but their horses refused to go until the holy icon was removed from the cart and thrown to

19

Parallel Roads (Lost on Route 66)

the ground. One of the men got so angry, he took out his sword and slashed the painting.

Mrs. Majewski was pleasant and friendly. She offered us some tea, which I accepted but Cheryl refused, being an avid coffee drinker. I could see Cheryl was anxious to see what we had come for. When Mrs. Majewski came back with a tray containing our beverages, she had the postcard. We looked at the front first. It was an aerial shot drawing of a drive-in motel. The caption read:

BROADVIEW MOTOR COURT
U.S. 54, Junction By Pass 66
SPRINGFIELD, ILLINOIS

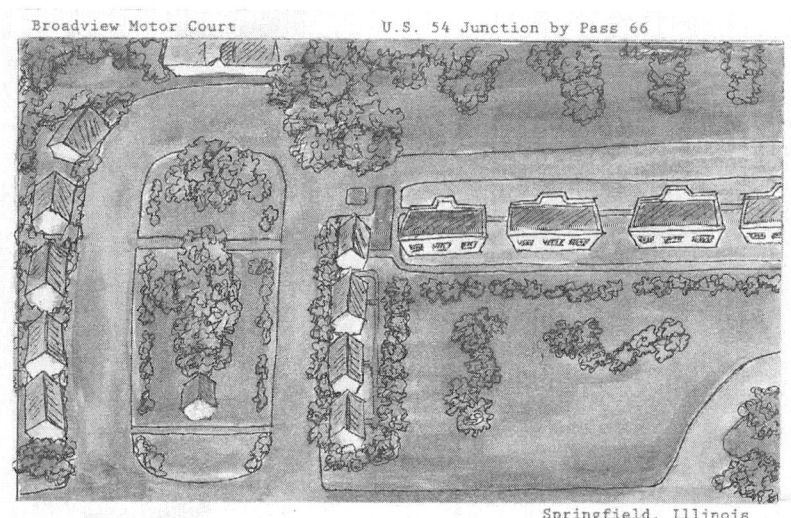

"What is Pass 66?" I asked.

"It doesn't mean 'Pass 66,' Kev," she answered. "It means it's located on US 54 and Bypass Route 66. It means your Grandma Kate, without a doubt, planned on taking Route 66 to Aunt Karen's."

Cheryl then slowly turned the card over and we saw my grandmother's handwritten scrawl.

Dearest Lidia,

I've been in dire straits these last few days. Need to sort things out. Should arrive in California by Friday. I miss John and little Sean already, and you, my dear friend. I hope you all can forgive me. Will talk to you on my return.

Love,
Katherine

The other side was addressed:
Mrs. Lidia Majewski
2790 N. Troy Ave
Chicago 27, Illinois

"I found the postcard while cleaning out my bureau. It was stuffed in with a bunch of cards and letters from my Teddy," Mrs. Majewski said.

Cheryl kept staring at the card. "Did she write any more? Could there be others here, ma'am?"

Mrs. Majewski answered, "I looked dear; I went through them all. This was the only one. I had forgotten she sent it. We all thought she would be back in a month. I even tried to talk to the foreman at the factory to keep her job open. They wouldn't because she never contacted them herself."

"Did you ever see my Grandpa John after this?" I asked.

"I ran into him once," Mrs. Majewski answered. "He was sad and anxious but told me how he kept busy with work and taking care of the baby, your father, Sean. He told me he was hopeful, that her postcards indicated her safe return."

"May I photograph this?" Cheryl asked our host.

"Take it with you, honey," she answered. "I hope it helps in some way."

"It could, ma'am; it really, really could," Cheryl replied as she gave Mrs. Majewski a hug. "Thank you so much, and please call if you remember or find anything else, anything at all."

We said our good-byes, and once we were back in Cheryl's Beemer, I asked, "How can that postcard help us any further? We now know that she took off down Route 66 and her first stop was Springfield."

"Kev, take nothing as definite. We don't know if this was her first stop or that she even stayed at this motor court. Maybe she did, but just because she has a postcard from it doesn't necessarily mean she stayed there."

"Well you're the Dick," I said, grinning.

"HEY, that's Detective Bachman to you, mister!" She continued, "We also know that Grandma Kate didn't plan on leaving for good. That was unclear from her good-bye letter to Grandpa John. So something kept her from returning."

"Okay, you're right," I said. "But you didn't answer my question. What further help can the card do us now?"

"Check out the top above her writing," she answered, pointing at the card.

I flipped the card over and looked. It had the AAA symbol and the name again as Broadview Motor Hotel, the address, and the phone number. "Hey, this phone number only has four numbers: 7636."

"Go on," she urged.

"Let's see, 'Approved, state inspected, AAA member, Best Western Motels, Extra Fine, None Better, Rest in Best.' Geez, they were corny back then."

"Keep going," she scolded.

"Oh, 'Witt Workman, Owner, and Mr. & Mrs. Lamar, Managers.' But wouldn't these people be dead?" I asked.

"Again, not necessarily. There could also be friends or family who might have old records. It was a Best Western–owned motel, so records could exist. I have work to do. Hey, I haven't read that good-bye letter from Grandma Kate in such a long time. Can we dig it out?"

1945–46
Chicago

"Kate!" John yelled as he rushed in the apartment, but seeing her face he stopped. "Are you all right, dear?"

"Oh, just a wee bit of morning sickness is all," she answered.

"I thought you were done with that. Doctor Butler said by this time morning sickness would be gone."

"Then perhaps it's something I ate," she quipped.

Changing the subject, John asked, "Who was that fellow I just saw leaving the apartment?"

"The Fuller Brush man. He wanted to sell us their latest line of brushes."

"Did you buy any?" John asked.

"No, John, there's nothing wrong with the brushes I've got."

John had never seen Kate is such a terrible mood. "Oh," he said, "I almost forgot. I have great news. Come look out the window."

Kate went to the window with John, and there parked right in front of the apartment was a brand-new green 1945 Plymouth Special Deluxe Coupe.

"What do you think, hon? Isn't she a humdinger? Dad bought it for us. He says it will be safer for us with the baby." John looked at her hopefully.

"Oh John, what was wrong with our old car? That's the car I learned to drive in."

John's demeanor turned serious. "I'm selling that old bucket of bolts as soon as I can find a buyer for it. Probably sell it for scrap metal. Besides, you can learn to drive this car. You'll love it, I promise."

Kate fell silent. She could see how proud John was of this new car.

* * * * *

Kate continued to drive the old 36 Buick around town until it became too uncomfortable to work the clutch in her delicate condition. The roads had also become very slippery that Christmas season. She almost slid right into the back of a pickup truck on Lawrence Avenue near Damen. The car stopped literally inches away.

One night she asked John if they could go downtown to see the Christmas lights and the window displays at Marshall Field's. Kate had loved Christmas ever since she was a little girl in Dublin. Before coming to America, she and her beau would go down to Arnott's and Cleary's for their annual Christmas window displays. Her fellow's name was Wayne Peterham. He had moved to Ireland from Manchester, England, at the age of eighteen to work in the agricultural surplus industry. They were young and so smitten with each other. Wayne promised to marry her as soon as he made enough money to ask for her hand. Wayne's family had money, but encouraged by his father, he wanted to make it on his own. His parents did not approve of his taking up with an Irish gal--and a Catholic one at that.

Wayne and Katherine were seemingly inseparable souls whose fate would eventually separate them when the O'Sullivan family set sail for Chicago in search of a better life. Katherine's young teenage heart was broken. Wayne vowed to follow her to the ends of the earth, but then came the news that he was killed in the Battle of the Bulge. She never fully recovered from her loss, the first of many in her life.

John was patient as Kate's disposition became more and more clouded and dark. But then one morning in mid-January, she woke up feeling on top of the world and started her nesting process. She got things in order, organizing the nursery she had set up in the spare bedroom. She ordered a crib from the Sears catalog, along with a basinet and music box that played Brahms Lullaby. She ordered diaper service and Bowman's milk delivery. She decided to order those new brushes from Fuller. She got herself ready, and for a time, life was as it should be for her and John.

Kate's timing was perfect, because on a cold Monday morning on January 28, 1946, Sean Michael Callahan was born at Ravenswood Hospital in Lincoln Square. He was a beautiful boy, born with black hair and blue eyes. Kate thought he was the finest Irish lad ever born in the New World. John was as proud as a father ever could be. Doctor Butler assured them both that little Sean was healthy and the chances of losing him were remote at best. He would grow to be a strapping young man.

"Look at him, Kate; we made that," John said to his wife the first time they looked at Sean through the nursery glass together.

"Don't be forgetting the good Lord now, John," said Kate.

"Yes, of course, dear," he answered. "I've thanked God already for this miracle of ours."

Kate grabbed John's hand. "I love you and I want you to know I always will. You'll make a fine father to this wee one."

"Thank goodness he has your looks," John joked. "I can't wait to bring the two of you home."

On the following Tuesday, February 5, John drove Kate and their new son Sean home to their Spaulding apartment. The Jacobsons met them at the door and offered a small chickpea dish and a Mazel tov blessing upon their heads.

In the days that followed, Katherine settled into the role of mother quite nicely. She loved bathing her sweet babe and reading to him. Her breasts were full to the brim with milk, and little Sean was plumping up quickly. But on the fifth day of being home, John noticed signs of melancholy start to return to his wife. Something was wrong, but he couldn't seem to drag it out of her. He took her to see Doctor Butler.

"She just has a bit of the blues," said the doctor. "It's quite common for women after the birth of a child."

"It's just that I worry so much after what happened the last time due to our loss," John fretted.

"Not to worry, Mr. Callahan," Doctor Butler reassured him. "That time she lost a child and you went off to war. This will pass, I promise you."

But it did not pass, and Katherine sank more and more into her darkness. She continued to take good care of her precious Sean but cared nothing for much else. They had the doctor's permission to reengage in sexual activity, but she wanted nothing to do with it or seemingly with John. He felt so helpless. He had no idea how to help her.

One night in March as they lay in bed together, John tried once more to find out what was wrong with his wife.

"John," she quietly said. "Have you ever loved so much it hurt?"

"You mean the way I love you?" John asked, trying to lighten the mood.

"I mean really hurt," she went on, "the way I love you and Sean and the others, too."

"Others? Which others?" he asked.

"Every one of them: Mom and Dad and Karen and Lidia and the Jacobsons and the people I left behind back home and the people who were killed in that bloody godforsaken war."

"Yes, I know what you mean. But, honey, we can miss them, but there is a time when we have to move on, when we have to live our own lives. If we don't, it's not fair to the people around us. Do you know what I mean, kitten?"

She fell silent for a while before replying, "Yes, I know exactly what you mean. I know what I have to do. Yes, John, I'll be taking your advice." At this, Kate turned over and they both fell fast asleep.

The next morning, John woke up for work as usual, but this would not be a usual morning. There on the pillow in which Kate's head should have been was a note.

Dear John,

Sorry, darling. I know the salutation sounds a wee bit cliché for a letter such as this. I am taking the old Buick and driving to California to see my sister Karen. I will drop Sean-o off at Mum and Dad's. You can pick him up after work.

I have to go, John. You were correct last night. Right now, it's not fair to the people in my life. It's not fair to you that I haven't performed my wifely duty, it's not fair to little Sean-o that his mum no longer laughs or smiles. There are things going on with me that I can't explain, that I can't tell you about. Things can't go back to normal until I've sorted it all out, and I can't do that while at home.

I love you more than you'll ever know. Please forgive me, my darling, and give my precious little man a big kiss from his mummy.

Love,
Your Kate

John ran to the nursery to find Sean missing, his bedsheet folded neatly at the foot of the crib. He ran to the phone and called his parents' neighbors, Mr. and Mrs. Flannery, since his parents didn't have a telephone. Mrs. Flannery came back with his mom who confirmed that Sean was there. She told him that Kate said she would be back for him later that afternoon.

"No, Mom, she lied. She went to California." John's voice was getting frantic. "Oh, my God, she's all alone out there with that old clunker of mine. My dear Kate, what has she done?"

Chapter 3
Two Thousand Miles All the Way

March
Present Day

"Wifely duty?" Cheryl asked mockingly, holding a copy of Grandpa's Dear John letter. "Grandma Kate was sure old-fashioned."

"It was 1946," I answered, "and she was from the old country. Besides, what's wrong with the idea of sex being a wifely duty?"

"Give me a break, dude," she quipped. "Why isn't it the man's duty, too? In fact, why does it have to be a duty at all? What's with this word 'duty'? Hey, you Catholics have that thing you used to call Easter duty."

"Yeah, where we are obligated to go to Confession and Communion at least once a year. So?" I answered.

"Well, if it's a duty, then she only had to have sex with him once a year."

"Very funny, Cheryl!"

"Hey, Kev," she asked, "where is the original of this letter?"

"I'm not sure, I've never seen it."

She continued, "Something just occurred to me about what Mrs. Majewski said.

She mentioned that Grandpa John told her he was hopeful because her postcards indicated her safe return. Don't you get it? There were other postcards from her."

"Holy crap! Do you think so?" I asked.

"Yes I do, we have to find those postcards!"

"Let's go see Grandpa John today instead of my planned visit this weekend," I urged. "We'll ask him."

"Do you think he'll cooperate?" Cheryl asked. "You know he doesn't like to think about things like that."

"Dunno, we'll have to just see what mood he's in."

We took Cheryl's BMW and jumped on the Edens Expressway toward the nursing home. The nurse told us that when my parents came next month, the home wanted to talk to them about changing Grandpa from assisted living to full-time care, that he had deteriorated in the past month. That made me sad. He didn't need any more losses in his life, and now he was losing even more of his independence.

Grandpa smiled when he saw us but had a faraway look in his eyes. I noticed a bandage on his left hand as I bent to kiss him.

"Hi ya, Gramps," I said. "What did you do to your hand?" He looked confused. "Your hand, Grandpa--what's with the gauze?"

"I burned it," he answered.

"How?" I asked.

He shrugged.

Cheryl stepped in. "Hi, Grandpa John." His smile broadened slightly. Even now, Grandpa liked the attention of a pretty girl. He always liked Cheryl and used to slip her silver dollars and candy when we were young. "Grandpa," she continued, "did you burn your hand on the stove?"

"Oh! Yes, I was making a can of soup," he finally answered.

I wondered why the nurse failed to tell us about this specifically.

"Do you think you'll be able to come to the apartment next month for Easter?" I asked.

"It's not Easter yet, Sean. Isn't it Christmas?"

"I'm Kevin, Grandpa, and Christmas and New Year's are over," I said. "But you're right, it's not Easter yet. Will you be able to come for dinner?"

He shrugged.

"We need to ask you something," I started. "It's about Grandma Kate." His face darkened and he got that far-off look again. "I won't say much about it. We just need to know if you saved her postcards."

"Postcards?" He looked puzzled.

"Yes, Grandpa, the postcards from her last trip," I said.

"I saved all her letters and cards," he answered.

"Where?" I asked. "Do you know where they might be?"

"I always keep Kate's things," he answered. "I bundle them and take them out and smell her perfume on them."

"Yes, Grandpa. Where did you keep them?"

He continued, "I brought her letters home from the war and saved them. The postcards came one at a time. I save them in the footlocker with the rest."

Ah yes, the footlocker. I remembered it now? "Do you know where it is?" I asked.

"We keep it at the foot of our bed," he answered.

I sighed because that bed was long gone, but I knew we had one chance and that was the attic. "Grandpa, listen. If we find the footlocker, is it okay if we go through it and read the postcards? We will take good care of them."

He nodded and waved his hand in a gesture that seemed like he was saying, have at it.

We stayed for quite a while more and tried to talk about happy memories. When we were saying good-bye, he grabbed Cheryl's hand.

"Is Kate home yet?" he asked.

"Not yet, Grandpa John," she answered.

After we left, I told Cheryl that it made me sad to see him like that. But when I told her I didn't think he was going to be with us much longer, she shushed me. So I set my mind on our new mission, and the minute we got back to the apartment, doing a lame Three Stooges impersonation, I pointed up toward the attic and yelled, "TO THE BASEMENT!"

As we started up the stairs, Cheryl retorted, "WHY I OUGHTA!"

We hadn't looked around up there in years. I only went up there occasionally to pull out Christmas decorations once a season and grab a suitcase now and again.

"Look at all this stuff! Kevin Callahan, don't you ever clean up in here?"

"What for?" I answered. "It's an attic. Look for an old brown case--that will be the footlocker."

"Some of this stuff could be worth a fortune," she said. "I could help you sell it on Craig's List or something. Look at this old clock . . . *oh,* and this tea set. Does this Victrola still work?"

"I don't know." I was only half listening to her. "I think I found it."

Once I saw it, the memories of it started flooding back. Cheryl ran over to me as I opened the case, and we both took in the old musty yet comforting smell of its contents.

I used to look at this case and wonder what mysteries it held. But I wasn't allowed in it when I was growing up. This is the first time I've ever looked inside. Sort of feels wrong in a way.

We carefully looked through the treasures and memories of a lifetime. There was a small pocket Bible with the clear inscription inside: John Callahan, 1941. Cheryl thought that he must have carried that with him during the war.

"Oh, my gosh, check this out!" I pulled out a shiny gold pocket watch, still on its chain. The cover was slightly worn and pitted. When I carefully opened it, I saw that the watch face and crystal were like brand new. The numbers and the name Elgin were clear and made with precise workmanship.

From Cheryl's vantage point, she could see the inside cover. "Look!" she said, gasping.

I turned the cover toward me and there was a picture of Grandma Kate. She was young and beautiful and happy. The picture was carefully cut out to fit inside the cover. I stared at it for such a long time. I had known pictures of her growing up, but none as beautiful as this one. Grandpa must have cherished it.

"Hey, look at this," Cheryl said, "a package." She was holding an unopened Parcel wrapped in brown paper and addressed to Mrs. Katherine Callahan. We looked it over carefully and saw that the stamps were skewed and the return address was from the Fuller Brush Company. The package was postmarked March 19, 1946. She must have ordered something and Grandpa John saved it for her return.

We continued to look through the footlocker. We discovered knickknacks that clearly belonged to Grandma Kate, plus other odds and ends. There was a scrapbook of newspaper articles about the war that Grandma must have started but never finished. One clipping had a photo of men lying in bunks being deployed overseas. But it's what we discovered under the scrapbook that made us stop dead in our tracks. There, lying at the bottom of this sarcophagus of memories was a bundle of cards and letters held together by twine. The postcard on top had Grandma's distinctive handwriting and was addressed to Karen O'Sullivan in

California. This was the one we knew about, announcing her arrival to Aunt Karen. Under it we could see a larger card with the stamp on upside down. It was postmarked, March 25, 1946.

"Geez, Kevin, they sure were haphazard when putting stamps on back then, weren't they?" Cheryl asked.

"No, this is cool," I said. "Remember that girl Rosemary I dated back in my sophomore year at St. Pat's? We used to do this, write letters to each other and put the stamp upside down because it meant I love you."

"But you didn't love Rose; she was just some cute girl you liked to have your arm around," she pointed out.

"That's not the point. She's the one who started doing this stamp thing, but when my friend, Jake, saw one of our letters, he knew what it meant, too. I'm just surprised they did it back in my grandparents' day."

"You still have that tendency to jump to conclusions," she said. "It could just be a coincidence. You saw how the Fuller Brush package had crooked stamps."

"Well, maybe, but look," I held up another card. "It's not upside down on Aunt Karen's postcard, nor was it on Mrs. Majewski's." We looked and saw that the stamps were pasted meticulously straight.

"Well," she answered, still not convinced, "let's go back downstairs and look at the rest."

"Okay, let's go. Hey, I'm hungry. Should I order from the Crust? The usual?" I asked as I made my way down the stairs again.

"The Crust" was The Golden Crust Pizzeria on the corner of Kedzie and Eastwood, and the "usual" was two thin-crust pizzas. One sausage and mushroom for me, one onion and mushroom for her. Although Cheryl wasn't as strict as she could be, she still followed kosher laws to an extent.

While we waited to go pick up the pizzas, Cheryl was still looking at the Fuller Brush package. "It feels like a book, not brushes. Could she have ordered a book from Fuller?"

"Open it, Cher," I said. "You know you're dying to."

Cheryl carefully unwrapped the paper, and we both sat there looking surprised at the old weathered book inside. We were even more astonished to see it was the classic *Gone with the Wind* by Margaret Mitchell. "What in the world!" Cheryl exclaimed. "The Fuller Brush Company did *not* sell this."

For the time being, we forgot about the postcards and letters, and started to page through the book. We saw that the book belonged to Grandma Kate and was well read and worn. It was inscribed with her name and the date of 1937. Then we came upon something so strange that all we could do was stare in blank confusion. There at the upper right-hand corner of page 614 was a three-cent postage stamp affixed sideways. Quickly paging through, she found two more stamps on page 322 pasted at right angles next to the page number. Cheryl finally looked up at me and I could see in her eyes that she now believed there was something going on with these stamps.

We put the book down to go get the pizza. We always went together because we liked talking to the worker bees.

"Remember when the Jewish bakery was right here next to The Crust?" she asked. "I miss that place. There's nothing like fresh hard rolls right out of the oven. It was my papa's tradition to buy them every Sunday morning."

Cheryl and I were perfect pizza pals. I liked the crust pieces and she preferred the middle. Thin-crust pizza in Chicago was cut in squares rather than the traditional pie shape. So when she was finished, I would eat all her crust pieces. I remember being in New York City for a train convention and going to a pizza joint near the Empire State Building. There they sold pizza by individual slices. I used the word "piece" as in, "I'd like a piece of your sausage pizza." The girl behind the counter looked at me like I had Mayor Daley written across my forehead. "Do you mean you want a *slice* of sausage pizza?" she asked. In New York, they fold their slices the long way, but it *was* fairly good pizza. I read once where both Chicago- and New York–style pizzas couldn't be duplicated elsewhere--it had something to do with the water. Sort of like sourdough in San Francisco.

I went into the front room to eat and ponder the book and stamps.

"What kind of pop do you want?" Cheryl called from the kitchen.

"Whatda we got?" I called back.

"We GOT," she said, mocking my Chicago accent that was much thicker than hers, "Mountain Dew, RC, and Diet Coke."

"RC," I answered, ignoring her mock. I wondered how it was that two people could grow up literally yards away from each other yet still talk somewhat differently. My words tended to have a lot of the dos and dats, such as, "Look at dos pigeons. See dat one over der?" It was just like the famous *super friends* from SNL, da Bears, da Bulls, da Cubs. While Cheryl hadn't lost her *th*'s as much, she said the word melk for what cows and other mammals produce.

After finishing and washing her hands, Cheryl went back to the book. Paging through it, she found a handwritten letter.

Dearest Katherine,

I received the message you left in this book for me. I understand completely but I feel it would be unfair to both of us if I didn't at least try one last time. Please meet me at Lou Mitchell's Restaurant. As always, the time and date are in the book.

I clipped the poem from the **Herald-American** *that I wrote for you. I posted it during my search for you.*

With love,
Wayne

Dennis Higgins

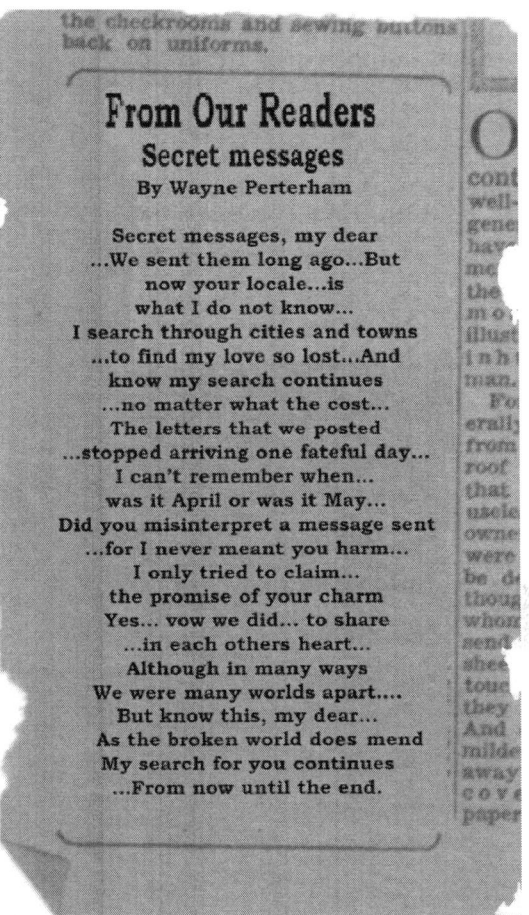

The poem read:

From Our Readers

Secret Messages
By: Wayne Peterham

Secret messages, my dear
. . . we sent them long ago. . . . But
now your locale . . . is
what I do not know. . . .
I search through cities and towns
. . . to find my love so lost. . . . And
know my search continues

. . . no matter what the cost. . . .
The letters that we posted
. . . stopped arriving one fateful day. . . .
I can't remember when . . .
was it April or was it May . . . ?
Did you misinterpret a message sent
. . . for I never meant you harm. . . .
I only tried to claim . . .
the promise of your charm.
Yes . . . vow we did . . . to share
. . . each other's lonely heart. . . .
Although in many ways
we were many worlds apart. . . .
But know this, my dear . . .
as the broken world does mend
. . . my search for you continues
. . . from now until the end.

    Cheryl was already on her laptop before I even finished reading it. She found that many newspapers of the time, such as the *Chicago Herald-American,* would often post poems, recipes, and other tidbits of information from readers during the forties and fifties. But she found nothing about Wayne Peterham.

    "Oh, my God!" I exclaimed, crossing myself. "Grandma Kate was having an affair. She ran off with him and probably lived out her life in Mexico as a bigamist."

    "Kevin, now just stop it," Cheryl scolded. "You have a very vivid imagination. We can only go by the quantifying facts; everything else is just perception. Now, here are the facts: We know that your Grandma Kate somehow gave this Wayne dude the *Gone with the Wind* book with some sort of message in it, probably having something to do with the stamps. We don't know what that message was, but according to his letter, it seems to be something he needed to understand. He indicated that he was still going to try. We don't know what that is, but the poem indicates that he searched for her and loved her."

    "But what about the meeting at Lou Mitchell's?" I asked. "Was that joint around back then?"

"Yes, of course it was," she answered. "Lou Mitchell's is a Route 66 restaurant. It's an iconic landmark. But remember that Grandma Kate never got her book back or that letter *or* that poem. It was still wrapped. We don't know that she ever made that meeting."

"We're going to have to finish this conversation in the morning," I said. "I'm tired and my head hurts. I need to go to bed."

"No problem," she answered. "I'm going to do a little more digging. Mind if I take the book downstairs with me?"

"Nope! Don't stay up too late, you night owl. Night!"

"Night," she called back.

Cheryl went downstairs and I crashed into bed. Sleep came quickly, as it had been a long, arduous day.

* * * * *

Early the next morning, I was at Cheryl's bed, shaking her arm. "Cheryl, wake up! Wake up, wake up, we have to take a trip."

"What the hell are you talking about?" she asked. "I could have been naked or something. Get out of my bedroom!"

"You sleep in jammies. Besides, I've seen you in your underwear before."

"Yeah, when we were, like, nine," she quipped.

"Look, Cheryl, this is important. We have to take a trip down Route 66."

"What? Route 66!" She was still dazed from sleep. "What are you talking about? It doesn't even exist anymore, at least as it did."

"Yes, but it can still be followed," I said. "I have a map."

"Okay, then--why?" she asked.

"I had a dream last night. It was not your ordinary dream. It was so real. I woke up believing that Grandma Kate was actually in my bedroom talking to me. I really believe she was." I started breathing hard and talking fast.

"Dude! Calm down! Now tell me about the dream."

I took a deep breath and started. "At first I was an observer. I saw Grandma Kate at that Lou Mitchell's place with a man I didn't know. They were talking quietly, sitting at their long table.

37

He was drinking coffee and Grandma looked upset. I couldn't hear what they were saying, but then I saw her put her face in her hands and start to cry. She then got up and started to leave but turned and said one last thing to him before walking out the door in tears. Cheryl, I never dream with this sort of detail. I even saw Milk Duds on the table for some reason. But then it gets even weirder. I was back in my bed and Grandma was right there at the foot. She told me that things were not as they seemed, that I had to follow her.

"So I asked her, 'What do you mean, Grandma? Follow you where? How?'

"But she basically repeated, 'Things are not as they seem. Follow my automobile.'

"Then she was gone and I was all alone again. I could see her. I could smell her perfume, hear her brogue. She talked like that *Touched by an Angel* girl. She was there, and we have to take a trip. I've already asked for emergency time off from the station. Can you take a week off?"

Cheryl stared at me for a moment and then asked, "Have you lost your mind? I work with facts, not dreams."

"I feel this is really important," I said. "This is real."

"Well I suppose there is some fact finding that can be done on location," she said, half to herself. "I will speak to my colleagues to see if they can take over my workload. I'm not into anything really pressing at the moment."

"YES!" I yelled.

"Whose car should we take?" she asked.

"Let's take mine," I quickly answered.

"Yours?" she asked, making a face. "But your car is so . . . how do I put this delicately . . . butt ugly."

"Well, I don't think it is. Besides, it's comfortable and has a kick-ass stereo."

"When do you want to leave?" she asked.

"Now!" I answered. "Get dressed."

"Go back upstairs, and I will be ready in about an hour. Where should we pick up the route?"

"I'd like to go to Lou Mitchell's," I answered. "Cher, I feel like I have a connection to her. I can feel her presence. I want to be at the places where she physically was."

A Cheryl hour is not the same as mine, so two and a half hours later, we were packed up in my black Chevy HHR. Personally, I loved its throwback simple looks. Sure, it wasn't a 500 Series BMW like Cheryl's, but it had some *get up and go.* Plus, it got decent gas mileage, and like I told Cheryl, it had a Blaupunkt stereo with monster speakers, a USB port, and a CD changer. I put in Wilco's latest and we were off for the Loop.

Chapter 4
That California Trip

March 22, 1946

Kate placed the good-bye note on her pillow as John slept and then gently picked up little Sean from his crib. Setting him down on a floor rug, she made his bed and neatly folded his extra blanket, placing it at the foot of the crib. She looked at the mantle clock and saw that it was half past four in the morning. After dressing the baby warmly, she quietly left the apartment only to find Wayne waiting outside by his car.

"What, pray tell, are you doing here, Wayne? Did you not understand the meaning in the book?"

Wayne answered, "Katherine, I had to come see you. Did you receive the book back? I posted it from work."

"No, Wayne," she answered, looking annoyed. "I did not get the book back. Now my husband will see it. That wasn't smart."

"I knew it wasn't, Katherine. I just felt so desperate."

"I can't talk to you here. John will be up soon and I have to go."

"Go? Where?" he asked.

"I'll be dropping off this wee one with his grandparents and then I'm taking a trip to see my sister," she answered. "I need to clear my head. I have a lot of thinking to do."

Wayne continued, "Katherine, I left you a message in our secret language to meet me at Lou Mitchell's on this very day. I had a feeling you wouldn't come, so I drove here. Please, darling, come with me so we can talk. Please . . . you owe me that much."

Kate thought to herself that it was a little out of the way but not that far from her in-laws place. It also was on Highway 66, so she could jump right on the road afterward.

"All right," she agreed. "I'll meet you for waffles, but I won't be a stayin' long."

Kate got into John's old Buick and drove down to North Kenmore. She felt a sharp pain of sadness while passing Wrigley Field. She knew how much John loved the Cubs baseball team.

She had so enjoyed going to the ballgame with him on a couple of occasions, watching him get so excited when Paul Gillespie or Paul Derringer hit a home run. She loved the excitement of the crowd, the smells, and the hotdogs. She knew that, with Wayne's background, he wouldn't know anything about these things.

While dropping off her little man, she had to hide her pain. She would miss him so much. She lied to the Callahans to avoid questions. If she had told them the truth, John's mum would try and talk her out of it. So she told them she would be running some errands and would return later. As she left the apartment, she parked a block away and sat in her car until her tears ran dry.

When she got to Lou's, she found Wayne waiting in the queue. The hostess handed her and all the ladies in line a box of Milk Duds. Once they were seated, the first thing Wayne blurted out was, "Katherine, my darling, I love you."

"You don't make this easy, Wayne. That's why I'm leaving. I'm in love with my husband and the wee one you saw back at the house, and yes, I love you too, dear Wayne. That's why I have to get my life sorted."

"But we made a promise to each other," Wayne said. "That promise meant something to me. You wrote for a time, and I loved getting those posts. The army and the war were hard enough, but then you just stopped writing."

"I thought you were dead," she answered. "It was in all the London papers. My relatives sent the articles."

"I was injured in the Battle of the Bulge," Wayne mussed. "I ended up in a small civilian hospital in Antwerp. All I could think about was you and how after the war I would find you. I know you're married, dear, and may God have mercy on my soul, but I need one last chance for happiness."

"Oh, Wayne!" she cried, cradling her face in her small feminine hands. "I am just so confused. Darling, please give me some time to think."

Like Scarlett O'Hara, Katherine loved two men, but unlike Scarlett, both the men in her life wanted to be with her. "I've got to go, Wayne."

"I may not be able to let you." Wayne's voice became louder. "This is NOT over yet."

Katherine Callahan got up and walked toward the exit, leaving Wayne sitting in his misery. Just before reaching the door, she turned one last time and calmly said, "You were my first, and I'll always love you."

The other patrons turned to look at her as she spun around and walked out the door.

Present Day
Lou Mitchell's

"I'm hungry," Cheryl said as she opened her box of Milk Duds. "I think I'll order the French toast."

"Those people are leaving," I said to the hostess. "Can we sit there?" I turned to Cheryl, "This is just about where Grandma sat in my dream."

"Coffee?" the waitress asked, already knowing the answer.

"Bless you, dear," said Cheryl. "Hey Kev, I found out more about that stamp thing on the Internet. I may have even cracked the code in the book. Apparently, the Victorians invented this secret language they used on envelopes, cards, and books to send messages without others knowing what they were. The trouble is that every country and time period had their own code. Just like spoken language, the language of stamps differed from region to region. It was so popular that messages were being sent this way all the time and were even used as espionage during World War I. Because of this, the universal postal services had to formalize the use of stamps on letters to the upper right corner. Before this, they could be placed anywhere."

"So how do you know what stamp language Grandma and this Wayne dude were talking?" I asked.

"Well, from the contents," she answered. "His message is easy because we know a few things. We know that Grandma Kate left on March 22. He put two three-cent stamps next to the page number 322. Get it, dude--3/22?"

"Cool!" I said. "But what about Grandma's message, the other stamp?"

"That one is harder, but I think I have it. The sideways stamp pasted on the upper right corner in the book could either mean 'Thinking of you,' 'Do not write me anymore,' or 'My heart belongs to another.' The latter is my guess, since I saw this meaning more in the British Victorian versions and also because of the page it was on."

"The page number again?" I asked.

"Nope, the words on the page. It's the part where Scarlett and Ashley are talking about the past opposed to the present. She tells him that she prefers the present, while he seems to be making a case for the past. I think the message was things were nice in the past but she prefers the present, and the stamp says, 'My heart belongs to another.' You see, Kevin, she loved Grandpa John."

I looked at the page. "It also says here that her mind pulled two ways."

After a great breakfast at Lou's, we went west to Ogden Avenue and on to Joliet Road, heading southwest. This was now Route 53, but back in Grandma's day, this was Route 66. Cheryl had put all the cards and letters in order by postmark so we could go through them with a fine-tooth comb. Once we got through Cicero, tornado alley of Plainfield and Joliet, it finally felt like we were leaving the Chicago area. It was exciting to be traveling the remnants of this defunct road that was once called America's Main Street. I turned down the radio and started singing the classic Bobby Troup song made famous by Nat King Cole. For a time we felt like it was a holiday and we truly were getting our kicks on Route 66.

Cheryl wanted to stop at Funks Grove for some of their famous maple syrup. I obliged her but was really only interested in being on the old road. The lady behind the counter looked at Cheryl strangely when she asked about the old town being haunted and, of all things, a Bigfoot sighting she had read about in the *Chicago Sun-Times,* but it seems the residents knew nothing about it.

Back in the car, I finally asked Cheryl what our first postcard was.

She grabbed the cards and told me there were actually two from the Broadview. The one we received from Mrs. Majewski and one to Grandpa John. I asked her to read that second one.

Dearest John,

I am writing this from Springfield. You don't have to worry, I am safe and the car is running fine. I have a companion to pass the miles away. Stayed one night at the Memorial Hospital. There weren't enough beds, so they let me leave. Just had to phone someone first to come for me. Give Sean-o a kiss from his mum. I miss you.

Love,
Kate

"You see now?" I blurted, slapping my hands on the steering wheel. "Maybe she did run off with that guy and my dream was nothing more than that--a silly dream. But yet I still feel something is wrong, like we're here on this mission for more than just truth finding. I can't explain it."

"Take it easy," Cheryl replied. "I've got the hospital up on my smartphone. Memorial Hospital of Springfield is now called Memorial Medical Center. It was started in 1897 by . . . hey, by my people."

"Snooty blonds with attitudes," I joked.

"Ha-ha! No, freak," she quipped. "By German Missouri Synod Lutherans."

"Excuse me. But may I remind you that your people were *not* Lutherans?"

"I meant German," she went on. "In 1931, it became non-denominational. It's on 701 North 1st Street. We need to go there, Kevin."

Walking toward the entrance door, you could see the old building as it was in Grandma's day. To the left and right were many additions and wings. As I got closer, I could feel my grandmother again, like I was walking next to her. It was early afternoon, and even though the sun was shining, I could see and feel the overcast day in which she lived as she entered the building. Cheryl did her thing at the information counter, showing documentation and pointing to me. After showing them my driver's license, the nice middle-aged woman finally came back with a CD that contained old transferred records. The woman searched for a time and then finally reported she had found it:

March 22, 1946, Mrs. Katherine Callahan was admitted for mild hysteria but was discharged after an examination by Dr. Gruber. Patient was suffering from hysteria following the birth of a baby. It was recommended that Mrs. Callahan phone a family member or friend before leaving the hospital care.

"Does it say who that person was?" asked Cheryl.

"No, dear," said the receptionist. "That's all there is. I hope it helps."

The information hadn't told us anything we didn't already know from her postcard, but yet it helped me connect with Grandma Kate in a way I couldn't even describe to myself. Getting back in the car, I suggested we drive over to the motel.

"Hey, Cheryl," I said. "What did you ever find out about the Broadview Motor Court?"

"Oh yeah, I forgot to tell you," she answered. "It was a bit of a dead end. Motor courts like this one were common along Route 66 and were really the forerunners of modern motels. That's where the word motel comes from, in fact: combining *motor,* as in drive up with your motor car, and *hotel.* Best Western didn't have records that went back that far. I did locate a Todd Lamar, who was the son of the managers. He said that the hotel business was his parents' whole life. They ended up owning their own Best Western until the day they died. But he could give me no further information about Grandma Kate."

We drove down Business 55, which was once Bypass 66, until we reached the corner of Route 54. Cheryl indicated that she didn't know which corner it was on, but I knew it immediately. It was there on the right side, where a Shell gas station stood. That was the old Broadview; I could see it in my mind. If only I could see her companion.

Driving away slightly disappointed, I suggested we stop for one of those famous Springfield Horseshoes. The Horseshoe was invented in Springfield, Illinois, and could rarely be found thirty miles outside the city. The Horseshoe started with ground meat: beef, pork, etc. It was then topped with French fries--and I mean a MOUND of French fries. Then the whole thing was smothered in gooey cheese sauce. The smaller version was called a Ponyshoe.

"Oy, I don't know, Kev. I'm not really interested in a heart attack right now."

We followed Business 55 until it met back up with the old Route 66 and headed out toward St. Louis. For a long stretch, we traveled the old road right next to I-55 on our left. I tried to fix my gaze toward the right. It was mostly farmland, with a couple of old towns that Grandma Kate would have passed like Divernon and Farmersville. Then we crossed I-55, which put the old route on our right. There were now signs for Litchfield, Mount Olive, and of course St. Louis.

Cheryl started to sing, "*Meet me in St. Louie, Louie, Meet me at the Fair . . .*" She did her finest impression of Judy Garland when she sang, "*We will dance the Hoochee Koochee, I will be your tootsie wootsie,*" Her voice went high on the word "wootsie" and I thought it was cute, so I joined in. "*If you will meet in St. Louie, Louie, Meet me at the fair.*"

Dusk covered the city as we neared St. Louis. I was thrilled to see the arch in the distance.

"Ah, St. Louis, Missouri, the gateway to the West," I said, "home of the blues, ragtime, jazz, Chuck Berry, and Budweiser."

"You bet, and don't forget the Cardinals. Didn't they finish in first place last year?" she asked.

"You had to remind me. The Cubs will win the pennant. Wait till next year." We slowly nodded in unison.

"Hey Kev, this is where Margaret and Bart went to school-- Principia. They are always telling us how beautiful it is in the spring."

"They're Christian Scientists, right?" I asked. "I wonder where the campus is from here."

"We haven't seen them in a while," she said. "Remember when we all went to the Music Box down in Lakeview for the *Grease* sing-along. That was fun."

"Hey, what was the next postcard from Grandma Kate? I just don't feel that she stayed long in St. Louis. I think she drove right past." Cheryl had already read all of the cards, but I wanted to hear them one at a time.

She pulled it out. "It's this one from Baxter Springs, Kansas. She may have stayed here. It's called the Capistrano Court."

Dearest John,

I miss my little Sean-o. I hope he is doing well and you are taking good care of him. Don't forget to read to him and rock him to sleep. We had a little car trouble in Missouri but have made it here to Kansas. Thought of you--I looked for Dorothy and the witch.

With all my love,
Kate

47

"She still used the word 'we,' as in 'We had car trouble,'" I noted.

"I'm trying to find Wayne Peterham," Cheryl answered. "The Fuller Brush company was quite helpful and they told me he did indeed work for them as a salesman from 1945 till 1953."

"So!" I replied. "If it was him on the road with Grandma Kate, he somehow returned to Chicago. Are there any more details about him?"

"Not really," she answered. "I have his address at the time. Naturally, he lived in Chicago--in the Logan Square area. Notes from Fuller stated that he moved from England and had experience in the sale of farming equipment."

"You hungry, kid?" I burst in, feeling my blood sugar drop. "Feel like Italian?"

"What are you thinking about?" she asked in a sing-song voice.

"We may not be staying in St. Louis, but we might as well take advantage of their good restaurants. Tony's is supposed to be one of the best."

Cheryl looked it up and found the address on Market Street, right across the river.

"No, I don't think that's the one we were told about. I thought it was closer to the old Route 66," I mused.

Cheryl continued to look. "Oh, I bet it's this one in Alton on Piasa Street. It's near the Chain of Rocks Bridge on the Illinois side."

We were still following Historic Route 66, which turned into the Chain of Rocks Road. As soon as I saw the old bridge, I stopped. The Chain of Rocks Bridge was now closed to cars and only used for bikes and foot traffic. Cheryl and I got out of the car. I felt Grandma strongly when I looked at that bridge. I knew Grandma had crossed the city this way.

Cheryl had her trusty 4G with her as always. The Chain of Rocks Bridge was built in 1929 to navigate across a rough part of the Mississippi river. The toll bridge was built with a 22-degree angle and was commissioned as part of Route 66 in 1936, but navigating it became troublesome, and in 1955, Route 66 was rerouted. The bridge was closed in 1967. "It's a beautiful old bridge, isn't it, Kev?"

We walked a way onto the bridge. The arch was visible to our left and the new bridge was to our right. I kept getting flashes, like memories but not my own. I could see the inside of Grandma's 1936 Buick and the presence of someone sitting in the passenger seat. I could feel thick sadness in the air. "Oh, Grandma Kate, where did you go? What happened to you?"

As we walked back toward the car, I had my head down, deep in thought, when I suddenly spotted something. "Hey, Cheryl, come here and check this out." I reached down and picked up a shiny Mercury Head dime. "You never see these in pocket change; someone must have dropped it from their coin collection. It's dated 1944. Hmmm, it's in great condition. They were still made of silver, you know."

"Yes, I know," she answered. "They quit making U.S. silver coins in 1965."

"That's my Cheryl," I said to no one in particular, "always with the facts."

Chapter 5
Go through Saint Looey

March 22–23, 1946

    Kate thought long and hard about who she should call to come for her. She had so hoped the hospital would have taken her in. She was told she could use the telephone in the small room where she was asked to sit. Should she call John? Should she try Wayne? No, they were partly the reasons for her departure. How could she pick one over the other? She removed the address book from her purse and paged through it. She found Lidia's number and dialed it. It rang and rang, but there was no answer.
    "Come on, pick up!" she yelled to phone's mouthpiece. With rising panic, she paged through the book. She came upon a Chicago number and an address that had been scratched and rewritten. The new address was in Decatur, Illinois. She dialed the number. After a rushed and desperate explanation by Kate, the voice at the other end explained that they would be on the next train to Springfield and should be there in about an hour and a half. She was also gently reassured and asked not to worry.
    Kate stayed in the little room staring at the walls. She couldn't read, and sleep was impossible. She sat still, with her own thoughts haunting her, until finally she heard muffled voices coming from down the hall. She listened as the nurse told someone that Mrs. Callahan was alright but distraught, and she was glad someone had come for her.
    As the voices grew stronger, the nurse was right outside her door saying, "She's right in here." The door opened, and there stood June Franklin, her old co-worker and nemesis from Bruning.
    "I'll leave you alone with her for a minute, Mrs. Franklin," said the nurse. "Come to the desk when you're ready." She walked away, her heavy white shoes echoing loudly.
    As soon as the door closed, Kate started to cry, and June went and put her arm around her.
    "Take it easy now, Katherine," she said. "Do you want to come home to Decatur with me?"

"No," said Kate through her tears. "I need to go see my sister, Karen, but I'm not at my best as you can see. Thank you so much for coming, June. I didn't know who to phone."

"Well, let's go find a place to stay for the night and you can tell me all about it, all right?" June helped Kate down the hall.

June Franklin was a tall woman in her early thirties. She had chestnut hair and a medium frame, and wore wire rimmed glasses. She didn't speak as eloquently as Kate's family or some of her other friends, and her clothes were plain yet pressed and clean. She was somewhat a hardened Chicago factory worker whose husband was killed late in the war. She had then moved to Decatur to stay with her dad and stepmom.

June led Kate out to the desk to fill out the paperwork and then escorted her to the car. "Let's just find a small place down the road," she told Kate. "But you'll have to drive since I never lernt how. Are you okay to drive, then?"

Kate's Buick ended up on Bypass 66. They pulled into the Broadview Motor Court and let a room for the night. The room was modest but nice and immaculately clean. The night air had a March nip to it, but the dwelling felt warm and safe. The ladies dressed in their night wear and sat facing each other, Kate on the bed and June in the room's chair.

"All right now, Katherine," June began. "Tell me what this is all about. Last I heard, your husband came back from duty and you were expecting."

Kate began, "Everything was fine when John came back. We were happier than before he left. I was with child right away, and life was good, June; life was just as it should be." She paused.

"So what happened? Did you have the baby?"

"Yes, I did. The good Lord gave Sean to me, my precious little angel. But I got sad right after the birth. Not just a wee bit sad, but a deep hounding sadness that I just couldn't shake. I felt I could have worked through it. My doctor said it would pass, that it was common. But then something else happened. My old beau from years before in Ireland came back into my life. I had heard he had died in the war, but there he was, standing at the door. He knew my situation, but he told me he still loved me"

"So why didn't you tell him to take a hike?" June asked.

"Because he was once the love of my life," Katherine answered. "He was the first to grab hold of this heart and he never let go. When my family moved to America, he vowed to find me and come for me. I made a promise also, I would wait for him. Seeing him there keeping his part of the promise...for a moment, I was swept off my very feet. For that brief moment, the new life I had with John and Sean was swept away and I wanted to throw myself back into Wayne's loving arms. But then I remembered the good life I had, so I told him to come back later, that I had to think things through."

"And?"

"I loved him, and I love my family. I felt like Scarlett O'Hara."

"Who?" asked June.

"Scarlett O'Hara from *Gone with the Wind*," Kate answered. "Did you not read the book or see the picture?"

"I'm not much for reading no books or seeing many picture shows, Katherine," June answered.

Kate continued, "Well, Scarlett loved two men, but it was always Melanie I related to. Melanie was nice and honorable. She was married to one of the men Scarlett loved. But Scarlett was really more in love with Scarlett than either of the two men, so she lost the both of them. That's how I saw it anyway. So I decided that I would not be like Scarlett but more like Melanie, and do the honorable thing and be true to my husband whom I love beyond words." Kate started to cry. "June, I really do love John. He deserves better than a wife whose heart is so divided."

June walked over to Kate on the bed and put her arm around her. "So what did you do about Wayne?"

Kate tensed but continued. "Back in Ireland, we were really just kids, you know. We used to play a game that was passed down from his family in England from Victorian times. We would write letters and have secret messages depending on how we placed the postage stamp on the envelope. Upside down meant 'I love you,' and tilted at an angle meant 'I can't wait to see you,' that sort of thing. We would also place them in books. What page or corner they were on or what the book was saying all meant something. It was easy once you got used to the code. So I placed a stamp in my book of *Gone with the Wind*. Wayne knew the love I had for that book. My message to him was, 'My heart belongs to another.' When he came again to my home, I handed him the book and closed the door. My heart broke in two at that moment, but I knew it was the right thing to do."

"So then you should have been happy again," June stated, "or at least happy that you had done the right thing."

"That's just the thing, I wasn't happy," Kate said. "The sadness was so great and I wondered about my life. How would it have turned out had I married Wayne and had *his* child? Back in Ireland, life was sweet and young. The promise of happiness all the days of our lives was ever present. I felt like life would never really change. We even faced the obstacles of our parents not being accepting of our love--he being English Protestant and my being Irish Catholic. But then my mum and dad lost the farm, and the only way to make a better life was to move to America. Of course, they took me with them and away from my beloved Wayne. June, it is so hard to forget him. It isn't fair to John and Sean-o to have a wife and mother who is there with only half her heart. So I had to leave. I need to go see my dear sister, Karen; she can always bring me back to my senses. She's a wise one, she is."

"Well, I'm not so wise," June said after a long pause, "but I think you should go back to John. He is your husband and the father of your child. I mean, I understand that you love this Joe from England and all, but geez, Katherine. If I had the chance to be with my husband again, I would take it. I wasn't always the best wife or person back before I lost him, and I'd take it all back to be able to see him again."

"I'm sorry for your loss, June," Kate said. "I know it must have been hard. May I ask you something?"

"Sure, go ahead," June answered.

"Why did you come to help me tonight?" Kate asked. "You weren't always the kindest person to me back at Bruning."

June stared at the picture hanging on the wall. It was a cheap print of a clipper ship harrowing a harsh storm at sea. She felt like this was how her life had been.

"I'm really sorry about that," June answered. "I was a bitter woman for reasons I'll keep to myself. But after I lost my Frank, something changed in me. I've never been much of a prayin' woman, but I think God wanted me to change my ways. I really did like you, Katherine; I just had a problem trusting women, especially if they were nice to me. I was also a bit jealous of you. Please accept my apology for everything I did and said."

"I'll be acceptin' your apology and as a Christian woman, I forgive you, but sweetie," Kate paused. "It won't be as easy to forget. But I also want you to know that it means a lot that you came for me. Now answer me this: why in heaven's name were you jealous of me? We were in the same boat, working in a factory to make ends meet while our men were off to war."

June answered, "I was jealous because you seemed so happy with life, because you had your faith and it showed, because you are so beautiful and . . ." she paused, ". . . because you never had a mother who drank herself to insanity, who showered you with love one minute and hated you the next, who called you vile names and beat you every other day."

"Holy Mother of God!" Kate exclaimed. She then put her arms around June and both women burst into tears.

After a while, Kate finally asked, "Would you consider coming with me? I thought I could but I don't think I can face the long journey alone. Oh please, June, come with me."

"All right, Katherine." Wiping the tears from her face, June started to laugh. "Or else you might pull me down by my hair again. That was the other reason I was jealous. You were stronger than me."

Both women laughed at the memory as Kate continued, "Life sure changed for us in these few short years."

Kate and June slept soundly. Kate woke up first at the crack of dawn. Going through the desk, she found a couple of postcards and wrote them out, one to John and one to Lidia. She always kept stamps in her handbag from her days with Wayne.

Once on the road, they found a nice café in Glen Arms for breakfast, and then it was back on Main Route 66 toward St. Louis. The miles passed quickly as the women reminisced about Bruning and Chicago. June told Kate about her mother and how she was institutionalized in Chicago's Dunning at Irving Park Road and Narragansett. In slang it was called the "end of Irving" because the westbound road went no farther. A neighbor had called the police when abuse was suspected. June loved her dad's new wife from the very first, but as it is with all women, she was unsure of her.

Kate talked about Wayne and about John and Sean and the baby she lost. There were small fragments of laughter but a lot of sadness and tears for both women.

"Can we turn this thing on?" asked June, pointing toward the radio. "Maybe we can hear some music or a good program."

"Sure, if it's still working," answered Kate. "I never play the thing, but John did all the time."

June turned the knob with a click and a hum came from the speaker as they waited for the set to warm up. She turned the knob past news shows, a sports show giving highlights from the Cardinals, and a Soldan High School basketball game. She stopped for a second to listen to a program called, "Ask Your Vet" on the *Ralston Purina Radio Show* until finally settling on a strong St. Louis station, KMOX, playing the Tommy Dorsey Orchestra.

It was almost noon when the women saw the St. Louis skyline. As they were not yet hungry and had just stopped for gas at Hamel, they decided to skirt the city over the Chain of Rocks toll bridge. Kate stopped at the booth and removed some change from her purse, accidently dropping a few coins to the ground. The attendant politely picked them up for her. Withdrawing the ten cents for the toll, he handed the rest back. "Enjoy your stay in Missouri," he said.

As Kate started across the narrow bridge, shivers went up her spine. She had the distinct impression that someone was watching her. She looked in her rearview mirror to see the toll attendant, but he was busy with other travelers. She navigated the sharp angle at the bridge's center and continued on to Missouri U.S. 66 toward Eureka and Allentown. June found it to be a very lovely stretch. The sign indicated that they were on the Henry Shaw Garden Way. There were all sorts of native plants, shrubs, and trees. But Kate was not in the mood for beauty just then. She simply couldn't shake the feeling that she was being watched, maybe even followed.

Missouri turned even more scenic west of the St. Louis area as the rolling hills of the Ozarks encompassed them. The women passed small towns and roadside stands, some selling mineral samples from the many mines and caverns across the state.

They finally decided to stop for a late lunch and gas up at the Marshfield Café, Phillip's 66. Kate still didn't feel much like eating but knew she had to try. She believed that June must really be enjoying the journey. She probably hadn't gotten to see as much of the world as she herself had.

When the hostess seated them, June was excitedly looking around the café and at the other patrons. She noticed a group of men, probably truck drivers, watching them. June wasn't used to men ogling her, so she was sure it was Kate who drew their attention. She crossed her eyes and made a face at them. The men turned, laughing to themselves. The couple behind them was discussing a news story they had just heard about the first U.S. rocket to leave the Earth's atmosphere yesterday. The man was saying that it was a complete waste of money and that Truman should put the kibosh on it.

June looked at Kate, who was gazing out of the window. "Hey, Katherine, where do you suppose we'll stop for the night?"

"I haven't a clue. I thought we would just drive until we were too tired to go on. As you saw, there are courts every few miles."

"Are you all right?" June asked. "Should we maybe stay here so you can rest?"

"I'll be fine," Kate said. "It may not seem like it, but I really am glad you're here with me. Sorry I'm not a wee bit more congenial."

"What's that mean?" June asked.

"I just mean that I'm sorry I'm not as happy and excited as you seem to be," Kate answered while placing her napkin on her lap.

"Oh, that's all right," said June. "I'm just glad to be here with you. I do wish you would look around at how beautiful these hills are, though."

Kate answered, "Every time I do, I think of how I wish John were here to see it with me. Then, at other times, they remind me of my home in Ireland and then of course, I think of Wayne." She looked at June. "I'll try and be more engaging for you, sweetheart."

June smiled, looking at Kate over her menu. "I have to tell you, Katherine, you still talk funnier than anybody I've ever met." Both women laughed.

The truckers got up to pay their bill. Comments such as, "Hey, good-looking" and "Hubba-hubba" were cast as they walked past the ladies. Kate ignored them and continued to gaze out the window, but June turned to look. One of the men stopped. He was what June would call tall, dark, and handsome. He wore a plaid shirt neatly tucked into his dungarees.

"Hey, doll," he started. "The name's Rocky. What do you say we blow this joint and go cut a rug?"

June looked closely through her glasses to make sure he was looking at her and not Kate.

Kate looked at June in time to see her face turn red as a beet. Turning to Rocky, she spoke on June's behalf. "No sir, I do not believe she does."

"Well, well. What do we have here?" Rocky asked, looking at Kate. "You Scottish or something? How about you, then? Me and the boys here are heading down to the Webster Hotel for a drink or two and some swinging." Looking back to June, he said, "Well, what do you gals say?"

June was still speechless. It had been a long time since a man had taken a fancy to her. But she knew Kate would never go for it. Still blushing, she said, "I'm sorry, sir, but we are not the sort of girls who can be swept off their feet at a roadside café."

Kate was proud of her and added, "Besides, can't you see? Tis a ring I be wearin'. We're meeting our husbands in a few minutes."

Rocky looked at her as if he knew she was lying. "All right, have it your way then, doll. Maybe we'll see you again sometime. Oklahoma is where I hang my hat, but we're up and down this whole highway every day."

The men left, and Kate sensed that June was tempted, so she warned her about the dangers of going off with strange men. Seeing the look of embarrassment on June's face, she added, "He *was* a bit of a looker, though, wasn't he?"

June nodded.

As they were paying the bill to leave, June grabbed a map depicting western Missouri, Kansas, and Oklahoma, so she could follow along. The car sputtered a little when Kate turned the key and then died, causing her to restart it.

Parallel Roads (Lost on Route 66)

Twilight and long shadows had settled across the old road as she pulled onto it. It wasn't long, however, before they were surrounded by the bright lights of Springfield, Missouri. Had they known they were so close to the bigger city, they may have stopped here to eat--although Kate thought to herself that the meal would have been far too dear for their pocketbooks. They stopped at a traffic light, and when she put her foot back on the gas pedal, the car shook violently.

"Oh, no!" she exclaimed. "I wonder if we got a hold of some bad gasoline."

Lady luck was with them, as they were near a service garage called Tarr's. The mechanic was just cleaning up for the evening. He must have had a soft spot for two women out on the road by themselves, as he agreed to look at the car. Having assessed the problem, he told them it would take about two hours to repair. Kate now really wished they had waited to eat. Just then, June spotted the Gillioz Theatre. The marquee read: "GILDA with Rita Hayworth and Glenn Ford."

"Oh, let's go, Katherine. Can we?" she pleaded. "It's been years since I've been to a picture show. It'll be my treat."

Kate had to smile at June's childlike excitement as she ordered popcorn at the counter with extra butter, a box of Goobers, and a Coca-Cola. She never imagined they would have a Saturday night on the town.

After the picture, Kate was starting to feel a little better, especially when she learned that the car wasn't going to cost too much to repair. The bill listed it as a clogged fuel filter and fouled plugs. Whatever that means, she thought. The mechanic assured her that the gas in the tank was good and only charged her fifteen dollars.

It was only about 8:00 p.m. and Kate knew that the hotels in town would be too expensive, so she decided to drive further into the night. She was pleased at how John's old Buick now purred like a kitten.

"Thanks for going to the show with me," June said as they pulled away and passed the Gillioz again. "I thought it was a good picture."

"Yes, I must admit, I rather enjoyed thinking about other people's lives for a time. I've never seen Rita Hayworth in a picture before. I guess I had her in my mind as a pin-up girl for the boys overseas. But she did a remarkable job, although I was sure she was going to lose her black dress during that Mame number."

"Katherine, can I ask you something?"

"Sure, what is it?" Kate answered as she navigated though the narrow streets of Springfield.

June went on. "I know I'm not pretty like you or sexy like Rita Hayworth . . ."

"What are you talking about?" Kate interrupted. "Of course, you're pretty. You just need to gussy yourself up a wee bit. I could help you with that."

"Don't be bananas, Katherine--all the gussying up in the world won't make me as pretty as you. But that man back there, Rocky, he seemed interested in me. Do you think I could ever find me another husband? I mean, Frank and I were both unpopular kids in school and we just sort of got matched together because nobody else would have us. After he went and got killed, I just assumed I would die an old maid. Gosh, I miss him though."

Kate paused before answering. She did not want to tell June she thought that Rocky was a complete swine. "Sweetie, I'm getting to know you in a completely different way these last couple of days. Tis a warm, wonderful woman with a young, enthusiastic heart, I'm looking at. That man back there saw that warmth shine through your eyes just as I do. That light makes you beautiful. June, look at me--I mean it. So, yes, I do believe you will find a man to marry and give you those wee babies you used to talk about when Frank got back from the war."

Tears welled up in June's eyes. "I'm not too old?"

"Heavens, no, what are you, thirty-five?"

"Thirty-three last month," June answered.

"Well, there you have it, then!" said Kate.

June turned on the radio, happy with the thoughts in her head.

"WMBH, Joplin," the announcer said, "Where Memories Bring Happiness. So now relax as we listen to Moonlight Serenade by Glenn Miller and his Orchestra."

But when the car actually reached the town of Joplin, Kate felt a shudder, as if she sensed a disaster on the horizon for this cute little town.

59

The feeling passed and after crossing the Kansas state line, the road took a southerly direction out of Riverton. By this time, it was nearly 10:00 p.m. and Kate decided that it was time to stop for the night. They entered the town of Baxter Springs and shared room 16 at the Capistrano Motor Court. Kate thought it was not quite as nice as the last place, but it was still clean and the bed was inviting.

That night, Kate had a strange dream. She saw herself, June, and a male stranger in a church pew. There was something familiar about the man, but she didn't really know him. At Communion time, he followed her up the aisle to the altar rail but did not kneel. After Mass, he followed them outside, and getting into a strange black car, he continued following them down the road. She wasn't afraid of him. Something about the man was comforting to her. Throughout the whole dream, he was invisible to June. When she last looked in her rearview mirror, she saw that there were, in fact, two people in the car.

Chapter 6
Oklahoma City is Mighty Pretty

Missouri
Present Day

Being it was a Friday during Lent, I couldn't have meat, but dinner at Tony's was still excellent. I had mostaccioli while Cheryl dined on chicken parmesan. We shared an order of their famous fried cheese ravioli. Cheryl and I left Alton and exited St. Louis via I-44 until Bourbon, where we were able to pick up the old Route again more easily. Even in the darkness, we noticed how Route 66 often paralleled the railroad track, which made perfect sense. The rails followed old Indian and settler paths, and Route 66 was built along the rails. Now the interstate followed the old Route as well, often constructed right next to or even on top of old U.S. 66. Portions of the new interstates were already being built in Grandma's time. It was difficult to follow the old Route through Missouri at times, as it weaved in and out with the interstate in almost a double helix pattern. But we did our best.

"So where to next?" asked Cheryl.

"We will follow our noses. Hey, did you get anywhere with the postcard from . . . where was it?"

"Baxter Springs, Kansas," she answered. "That turned out to be a dead end as well--so far at least. The Capistrano Court is long gone and no records are available. I do have some police reports that I'm waiting for."

"Police reports!?" I asked.

"Sure thing," she answered. "We don't know what happened to Grandma Kate. Police records and newspaper reports from the local areas could tell us something. I can get some reports electronically, but others will require us to physically hunt for them at libraries and police stations"

I thought about this for a moment before asking, "But if something bad happened to Grandma, like maybe this guy Wayne killed her in a jealous rage, wouldn't you only need a police report from somewhere *after* her last known location?"

"Not necessarily," she answered. "Small things in small towns were often big news. Sure, it's all a long shot, but I have to cover all the bases."

"Nice baseball reference, Cher. Hey, I'm getting tired after that meal. You mind driving for a while?" I asked.

I settled back in the passenger seat and relaxed. Looking out the window, I imagined my grandmother driving this very road over sixty years ago. As I let my mind wander, I found my thoughts turning to Cheryl. It's funny--here we were just on the other side of thirty years old and neither of us had ever married. We both had our share of dates over the years, but after each one we would come home and call the other to give or get the scoop. In fact, if I got tickets for a play at the Shubert Theater, it was Cheryl I would think of taking. Same with her and the free Cubs tickets she always seemed to score. I often wondered if our close friendship kept us from something more permanent. But neither of us ever talked about it.

I admired her so much. I remember the day she told me she was training to become a cop. My best friend, a Chicago police officer--I just couldn't believe it. But she turned out to be a good one. She spent a couple of years on the force, but she was only logging hours for what she had really wanted to do, which was to become a detective. She finally took and passed the test at the Illinois Department of Financial and Professional Regulation. That night we had celebrated with a bottle of Dom Pérignon and Carson's Ribs down on Wells Street.

Our friends couldn't understand why we'd never hooked up romantically. I was sure they thought it was our religious differences, but it wasn't. We loved each other dearly. We just didn't love each other in the Eros way but rather the Philia. That was to say, we loved each other like brother and sister. Both of us were only children, but our friendship went far beyond even that. Cheryl was currently seeing the nephew of her rabbi, a guy named David Levinson. But I surmised that it couldn't be that serious since she left town to go on this adventure with me.

My thoughts dissipated into sleep until I woke up with that increasingly familiar feeling of being close to Grandma Kate--as if her energy were concentrated all of a sudden. "Where are we?" I asked groggily.

"I'm still following the old road," she said. "We crossed I-44 at Phillipsburg. That was about a mile back."

I got out the map and looked. We were on County CC. The next big town was Marshfield. Just seeing the name, I knew there was a connection with this town and Grandma Kate. Cheryl wanted to stay and check it out, but I didn't feel that the town held any real importance to us, just that Grandma had spent some time here.

As we drove down County CC, it became evident that any business that was once here on Route 66 was lost forever when the new interstate re-routed traffic around the town. I urged Cheryl to drive into Springfield, Missouri. Cheryl agreed, since it was close enough that she could gather any info from there.

Springfield was a quaint old town and had that feel like we were really starting to be in the West. It was evident that the town took pride in its preservation of the past. As we stopped at a red light, I thought I felt the car shutter, but Cheryl assured me it was just my imagination.

"Grandma also spent time here," I told her. "Check out that old theater. Hold on, stop!"

Cheryl stopped the Chevy in front of the Gillioz Theatre. I jumped out and stood, staring at the red front doors, fingering the Mercury Dime in my pocket. In my mind, I could see a ticket booth in front of them, but in reality, there was none there. I felt a sense of happiness. Cheryl came around and joined me.

"Grandma Kate must have attended a play or movie here," I said.

"Why do you say that--are you having that so called feeling of her presence again?" Cheryl asked.

"Yep, and strongly, too. This place gave her joy," I answered. "It's the first time I've felt that emotion in connection with her. What do you suppose she saw here? Did that Wayne dude take her on a date?"

Cheryl frowned at me. "May I remind you, Mr. Callahan, that we have not established for sure that her companion was indeed Wayne Peterham."

"So tell me this. If he went back to work at Fuller until the fifties, why can't we find him?" I asked. "And when I say *we*, I mean YOU!"

"My guess is he returned to Ireland, but I haven't had any luck tracking him there either," she said. "I'm going to expand my search to the rest of the UK. Come on, let's boogie. We're illegally parked."

"I would really like to know what show she may have attended here," I said as I started back toward the car. "I know it's not really important, but I really want to know."

"Let's see what we can do in the morning," Cheryl said. "It's getting late. I figure we can spend all day here tomorrow."

We booked two rooms at the La Quinta Inn. As we took our suitcases out of the car, Cheryl hit me with one of her facts. "Did you know that Kathleen Turner was born in this town?" I did not know that.

The room had free high-speed Internet, so I was finally able to check my e-mail without bothering Cheryl to use her phone or laptop. There was one from my dad telling me about some Ed Sullivan Rock and Roll special on PBS. I gave him a heads-up about Grandpa John and what the nursing home told me--how they were going to talk to him in a couple days when he got to the city. There was one from our friend Diane. She and her new boyfriend, Jack, wanted to hook up for a play at the Biograph Theater. This place had gone through transitions over the years since public enemy number one, John Dillinger, was shot outside of it. My grandparents saw movies there, my parents went to midnight showings of *The Rocky Horror Picture Show,* and now it was part of Victory Gardens, showing all sorts of contemporary plays. I shot off a couple more e-mails and went to bed.

The next morning, we enjoyed La Quinta's Bright Side Breakfast, which was actually pretty good, with homemade waffles that you cooked fresh yourself.

Afterward, Cheryl and I headed to the library, where I let her do her thing. She also made arrangements to meet a representative at the Gillioz. I watched as she rifled through newspapers on microfilm. There was nothing of significance on the dates in question from either Marshfield or Springfield. The March 23, 1946, police report indicated that a fight broke out at the Webster Hotel in Marshfield when an intoxicated man named Rocky, no last name, tried to dance with the hardware-store owner's wife. Three men spent the night in police lockup, and the woman was treated for minor cuts and bruises. Cheryl searched the papers for the movie showings, but there were none.

We were almost late for our appointment at the Gillioz. We rushed into the splendor of this magnificently restored theater. A pleasant, middle-aged woman met with us. She introduced herself as Sharon and told us that she kept records and also had a personal interest in the history of the Gillioz. We learned that it opened its doors on October 11, 1926. It had a pipe organ, for live performances and silent films. We were also treated to the fact that one month later Route 66 was born just next door at the Woodruff Building, where the U.S. Secretary of Agriculture officially approved the Federal Interstate Highway System and numbered it 66. Due to this fact, they called Springfield the birthplace of Route 66.

We asked her why we couldn't find a newspaper ad for the Gillioz on microfilm for March of '46. Sharon told us that in small towns back then, everybody knew what was playing from the marquee. They would often see the same movie over and over just for the changing newsreels. She looked though her records and told us that premiering on March 15, 1946, and running for almost two months, was the movie *Gilda.*

We decided to skip lunch and have an early dinner instead. Cheryl discovered that the southeast corner of Springfield seemed to have a concentration of Mexican and Southwestern restaurants.

We always liked to find good local cuisines rather than chains, although Springfield was quite a cosmopolitan city, with everything from Italian and Asian to eclectic American. We settled on a place called Coyote's Adobe Café on Glenstone Avenue, mainly because their claim to fame was chicken wings.

We decided we would stay overnight and get an early start in the morning. So this meant we could relax and have a couple margaritas, wings for appetizers, and some authentic fajitas. The place had a nice atmosphere. Their Saturday-night crowd had mostly come to watch the Rams game.

After dinner, we were actually able to find *Gilda* in a video store. Since we were from out of town, they wouldn't let us rent the DVD, so we had to talk them into selling us their copy. They ripped us off, of course, but this allowed us to go back to one of our rooms and watch it.

*****

"Oy vey, I can't believe how beautiful Rita Hayworth is in this movie," Cheryl said as we were nearing the end.

"Tell me about it," I said. "She was downright HOT!"

She nodded and added, "Glenn Ford was no slouch either."

I just shrugged. "If you say so, Cheryl. But neither of them were very nice people. Why do you suppose my grandmother enjoyed this movie so much?"

"Not really sure," she answered. "Probably just to step out of her own life for a while by stepping into theirs. I always imagined that's how movie goers did it in the forties, especially during the war. They would watch great dramas, love stories, and comedies with lots of singing and dancing just to forget about the problems and worries of the world."

"We've lost that, haven't we?" I asked. "I mean, we're so used to seeing movies. Hell, we can download them, stream them or even rent them from boxes for a buck. But back then, seeing those glamorous people bigger than life must have been a completely different experience."

It was great watching the movie while we were still here in Springfield and the Gillioz was still fresh in our minds. It made the connection I had with Grandma Kate that much stronger.

The next morning, I wanted to get on the road early. It was Sunday, but I had forgotten to have Cheryl look up the churches in town for me. Besides, we were leaving before the first Masses of the day. I hoped to stop later if I saw a Catholic church. We headed out of Springfield on State Highway 96 toward Carthage. This was one of those towns that completely got skipped by the interstate. Carthage had a rich history, with Civil War battles and a beautiful historic courthouse. It had been home to a notorious female bandit called Belle Starr. As we drove through, we could see that the town still catered to Route 66 enthusiasts. It was strange how the road itself often became a huge part of a town's history.

We drove on past Carterville, Webb City, and Joplin, which still showed signs of the horrific tornado that devastated it a few years back. This finally brought us to the Kansas state line. At Riverton, we took a southerly turn on Route 69, which was the old 66, toward our next destination of Baxter Springs. Even though Cheryl had told me that the motel Grandma Kate had sent the postcard from no longer existed, I felt a strong connection here. Many towns were bypassed by the new interstate, but here the entire state of Kansas was skipped. I was impressed that Baxter Springs seemed proud of their old connection to Route 66.

I wasn't sure why, but I instinctively made a left turn at 12th Street in town. That's when I saw it: a small little red church called St. Joseph's. As luck would have it, people were gathering for

Mass. I asked Cheryl if she wanted to join me, but she declined, saying that she would drive around town and scope out a place for breakfast. I wouldn't have even known this was a Catholic Church by the look of it. It was a far cry from the beautiful Gothic and Romanesque churches of Chicago, yet this little church had a spirit-filled atmosphere full of love and peace. As I approached, I felt that Grandma must have been here, but there was also some sort of disconnect somehow. I couldn't explain it. It was like Grandma Kate was here yet she wasn't. The congregation was a mixed group. There were Asians, Caucasians, and Hispanic peoples. The presiding priest was Asian, but the Mass was in English. I felt people were looking at me because they weren't used to visitors. They were warm and friendly at the sign of peace, walking across the aisle to shake my hand with a smile and a "Peace be with you." I felt Grandma's presence strongly at Communion time. In my mind's eye, as I had started calling it, I saw her go up and kneel to receive the host.

After Mass, the priest greeted the people outside. He received me warmly, asking me where I was from. I discovered that he was the only priest serving four different churches in the area. He was born in Burma and came to the United States in 1994.

Cheryl pulled up and slid into the passenger side as I got in. "I found a great-looking place for breakfast right down the street. It's called the Little Brick Inn."

"Cool!" I said.

"How was church?" she asked.

"It was really good. I'm glad I went to this one. I know Grandma Kate was there. But I felt something I can't quite explain. It was like she was there but at the same time not exactly."

"If there's any truth to this connection of yours, I may be able to explain that," she answered. "I looked up the church while I was waiting."

"Oh, really?" I asked as sarcastically as I could.

"Yes, really," she answered, ignoring me. "The physical church was built in 1917. It was picked up and moved twice before ending up where it is today. The last move was in 1946, probably after March."

"So my grandmother went to this church, but it was in another location?" I asked.

"Yep!"

"Okay, smarty pants," I said. "So how come I knew the church was on 12th Street?"

"That's because the old location was also on East 12th Street back then too. I couldn't find the exact spot, but since East 12th Street isn't that long in Baxter Springs, it was probably moved no more than a block or two, maybe even yards."

"That does explain it. Thanks, kid," I said.

"No prob," she replied, sounding proud of herself. "I knew you'd come to appreciate my mad skills."

"Yeah, yeah," I said, smiling.

I looked around inside the Red Brick Inn. The place was old and nicely restored as a café. Apparently, back in the 1880s it had been a bank. Legend had it that it was once robbed by Jesse James.

After breakfast, we got back on the old road heading right for Oklahoma. Getting tired of singing Rogers and Hammerstein with Cheryl, I finally put on a CD by the Decemberists and we started to settle in for the long drive across the Sooner State. Oklahoma had nice long stretches of Route 66.

"What's the next postcard?" I asked.

"Here it is. It's a generic one from here in Oklahoma. I'll read it. Hey Kev, this one has the stamp upside down. I wonder if Grandpa John knew the code. It's postmarked March 26, 1946."

My Dearest John,

We didn't visit any of the places on this card. The road here in Oklahoma is difficult to travel on at times. Was forced to stay east of a flooded river tonight. Have decided to make my visit with Karen a quick one. Tell Sean-o his mummy loves him. I love you too, John.

Love,
Your Kate

"The tone was different in this one, wasn't it?" I noted.
"That's what I thought," she answered. "It's just like your Grandpa John always said, that it seemed like she was coming back home, although she never said it directly."
"So where do you think she wrote that from?" I asked.
"It's hard to say," she answered. "There are lakes and rivers throughout Oklahoma. My best guess is the South Canadian River, which according to Internet sites had a history of flooding."

"So where is this river?" I asked.

"Clear across the state. "We have a long haul ahead of us."

"What's the date, Cheryl?"

"March 27, why?"

"It's too bad we didn't link the date for our trip up more closely with Grandma Kate's trip. We're what, three or four days off?" I asked, counting on my fingers.

"Do you think that's important?" she asked. "The days of the week this year don't match with 1946."

"Naw, it's probably not important," I said. "Good point about the days of the week matching. Actually, I believe my grandmother and I were both in that church on Sunday. So we are linked that way, for now anyway."

Cheryl had no clue that the real reason I was asking was because I knew tomorrow, March 28, was her birthday. I could tell she thought I forgot, and Cheryl was not the type to say anything. She had always been that way. I remember that she was hurt on her twelfth birthday, when due to the excitement of her Bat Mitzvah party, I had completely forgotten that it was also her birthday. I made sure she got a Bat Mitzvah present. Her mom had told me it would be nice if the gift represented the number eighteen in some way. I didn't know what to buy, so I wrapped up eighteen Pixie Stix, along with a little gold Star of David my parents bought for me to give her. I couldn't help it--we were into Pixie Stix. Like I said, she was hurt but she still wore that Star or David around her neck to this very day.

This year, I was planning to surprise her with tickets to see They Might Be Giants at the Rosemont Theater. I had the tickets with me, but I still needed to stop for a card.

Driving along U.S. 60, we came to a famous Route 66 site, but not one that would have existed in my grandmother's time. However, the Blue Whale of Catoosa was still a great sight to see. It was built in the 1970s and was once part of a water park with a zoo. Cheryl told me how the park was closed in the 1980s, but residents of Catoosa, with the help of the Hampton Inn, restored the whale. It was a true Route 66 icon.

In Vinita, we passed another old Route 66 landmark, a diner called Clayton's Café. I had seen it featured on a TV show. It was too bad we didn't have time to stop--it would have been there in Grandma Kate's time.

Moving on finally brought us into Tulsa, which reminded me that I could probably find some good radio stations around here. However, I was surprised at the lack of stations that matched our musical tastes. Amazingly, the first half of the FM dial seemed to be all contemporary Christian or gospel. Plus there were several classic rock and oldie stations that my parents would have loved. I finally settled on Z-104.5, The Edge, which was a mix of modern rock and alternative.

The old Route 66 went straight through town via 11th Street. As we crossed over the Arkansas River, I could see the old 11th Street Bridge and I just knew Grandma Kate had crossed there. Soon we were back in alignment with the old road through Sapulpa. The interstate I-44 would be right next to us from here to Oklahoma City. I came to hate that impersonal monster road with its tolls and speed traps. We had to cross right over it several times and even had to jump on to bypass the city for a short time. Although they were very serious and important, signs along the way that read DO NOT DRIVE INTO SMOKE made us chuckle. It was something that we just had never experienced, being city dwellers all our lives.

I got the feeling Grandma Kate also took an alternate route around Oklahoma City, but the exact roads she used were unknown to us and may no longer be in existence.

Once we took the Yukon Exit, we were back on the old road toward El Reno.

It had started to rain and the sky grew dark, but we had a nice long stretch of Historic Route 66, with signs clearly marking the road. When we crossed the Canadian River--which Cheryl guessed was the site where my grandmother got stranded--I got a dark sinking feeling. I felt like something bad had happened here. Maybe I was just feeling Grandma Kate's stress of not being able to cross.

The radio went to static as we reached a place called Hinton Junction, which had a park right off the road. I pulled in to rest since the rain had turned to a downpour. I could see lights on in a café down the road and a brick gas station.

I felt a connection with Grandma Kate as we sat there with the rain beating on the car, but I felt like I had lost her path. She was never here, which was strange because we were directly on Route 66. I set my concentration high, trying to feel her presence. I looked toward the road and could see a few headlights passing. I strained to look closer as the next car passed and saw it was an old antique vehicle. The taillights were so small and dim, I wondered if it was street legal.

"What do you suppose happened to the radio?" Cheryl asked.

"I dunno," I answered. "Probably has something to do with the storm."

I flipped the stations and got nothing on FM, so I switched to AM where I found some old Grand Ole Opry–type country music, more Gospel, and an old bit by Jack Benny and Rochester. I hit the button and turned it off.

The rained slowed only slightly, and I decided to get back on the road. All at once there was a flash of lightning that must have been right in front of the car. Cheryl screamed and I was blinded for a second or two. When I regained my vision, I had to slam on my breaks to avoid hitting a Toyota Camry that was right in front of us.

"Where the heck did he come from?" I asked. "Did you see that car there before the lightning?"

"No," she answered. "The road was clear."

The road became really bad with gravel and flooding, but we mustered through and decided to stop at the next big town, which was Clinton. Right after Weatherford, we made the decision to jump on I-40 with the old road right next to us. We exited at Gary Avenue, and I immediately felt that we had linked up with Grandma Kate's route again, but we were down for the count, at least for that night. We decided to stay at the Hampton Inn on Lexington, since along the way we had learned that they were pro-Route 66 preservation and had helped fund many Route 66 projects. Here in Clinton, they heavily promote the Route 66 museum just down the street. They also promote the Native American culture that was so prevalent here.

Behind the counter was an elderly, talkative gentleman. "Howdy, folks, welcome to the Hampton Inn," he said. "Bad storm tonight. We never get mild rains in this part of Oklahoma, only downpours and flooding. I know 'cause I've lived here all my life. Retired over twenty-five years ago but just couldn't stay put doin' nothing. I help out here a couple nights a week. The name's Sam. Young people don't like to work the night shift, too many things going on, so I help out. Yup, that's a bad storm."

"Yes sir, it is," I answered. "We had to stop for a while at the roadside park."

"And what roadside park would that be young fella?" Sam asked.

I looked at Cheryl and she answered. "It was called Hinton Junction. It had trees and some stone picnic tables."

"Hinton Junction!" Sam said, looking bewildered. "Why I haven't heard that crossroad called that in years. Used to be a nice park there, yup, but not now, not for thirty, maybe forty years. Barely anything there now. Back then it was a rest stop along good ole Route 66. The new highway changed a lot of things. I was originally from Bridgeport--darn near a ghost town now. Used to work in Geary as a mechanic and a tow-truck driver. It's still there, but at one time the old Route went right through Calumet, Geary, and Bridgeport. They moved the road away. I mean, some highway workers just came and took down the signs, bypassed all three towns. That was back in the thirties. Yeah, I'm that old. Wouldn't know it to look at me though, would ya? Where you kids from?"

"Chicago," I answered.

"Never been there," Sam said. "Too big. Never even been east of Kansas my whole life. You folks have a nice night now."

Once I got settled in my room, I went over to see Cheryl who was at her computer.

Before I could say anything, she beat me to it. "What the hell, Kev! What does he mean there's no park there? We know there's a park there."

"Yeah, I know," I answered. "The guy seemed to know what he was talking about, though. We'll ask around in the morning."

"Kevin," she answered, her eyes never leaving the computer screen. "Here's the weird part. I searched for Hinton Junction on Bing.com and it came up with a couple of Flikr pictures taken by someone. Dude, it isn't the park we saw last night. It's basically abandoned. The café and gas station we saw are also abandoned. That's not all. The only other references to Hinton Junction are from book reviews from the thirties and forties."

Back in my room, as I unpacked and separated my dirty laundry, I found Grandpa John's pocket watch. I had forgotten that I even packed it. I opened it and looked at my beautiful, youthful grandmother's picture. "What could have happened to you, Grandma?" I said, staring at the watch.

I laid it on the desk with my keys and wallet. I decided I would wear it tomorrow instead of my Timex.

The next morning, I woke up early and asked the girl behind the desk where the closest Laundromat was and if I could get more coffee for my room. Cheryl met me there at the front desk, also in search of coffee. The girl pointed to a courtesy coffee urn set up in the lobby. "Bless you, Miss," said Cheryl as she made a beeline toward the cart.

As we sat in chairs sipping our coffee, a manager asked us if everything was all right.

I took the opportunity. "May I ask you something? The older gentleman at the counter last night . . ." I began.

"Oh, you mean Sam," the manager interrupted. "Sam Taylor. Yes, he's quite a character. What about him?"

"He told us there was *not* a beautiful roadside park at Hinton Junction," I replied, "but we were sitting there in the rain last night."

"Hinton Junction?" he asked. "You mean where Highway 281 meets Route 8?"

"Yes," Cheryl and I said in unison.

He went on. "There are a few lights and a couple of tables. It's not really set up to be a park."

"Are they stone tables and do they have fireplaces?" Cheryl interjected.

"Goodness, no!" he answered. "I think it used to be like that before they built the interstate. The whole area is in disuse, except by local people."

Cheryl continued, "What about the café and gas station? We saw lights on."

"Now *that* would be impossible, Miss," he said. "Used to be Leon's place, but it's been gone for years."

We thanked him, and as he walked away, I looked at Cheryl and asked, "What does it mean?"

"It means," she answered, "guidepost up ahead. We have entered into . . . the Twilight Zone."

Chapter 7
You See Amarillo

March 24, 1946

June tagged along with Kate when they found the little church of St. Joseph's in Baxter Springs. When she was a kid, her parents would sometimes take her to the Methodist church. Having the service in Latin was not something she was used to, but she told Kate she liked what the priest had to say in his homily. It was about the war being over yet how people were still at war with each other back home. He talked about how they should clear their hearts and their minds of evil, and make peace with everyone as well as themselves--to truly embrace peacetime.

Kate thought that the little church surely reminded her of the dream she had the night before. She looked around to see if she could find the stranger but saw no one. Yet the feeling of the dream and that man was so strong with her. Did he represent John somehow? It felt like he was a part of her in some way.

After Mass, they headed back out of town toward Oklahoma. They started to notice that the soil was turning a red color. June switched on the radio, and the women were treated to the songs of Tulsa's favorite, the Texas Playboys.

The road took them right through Tulsa on 11th Street. Kate thought there was quite a bit of traffic for a Sunday, yet she felt at home in the big city. There were many large downtown buildings, just like Chicago. Oh, how she missed John.

She stopped for gas at a Mobile Oil station and admired the neon sign from the building next door. As the attendants filled her car, washed her windows, and checked her oil, the Meadow Gold sign made her think about whether or not Sean was getting enough milk.

"Where you ladies headin'?" the attendant asked when she handed him the money.

"California," Kate answered.

"Well, you can make it in two or three days, but you best be careful 'cause I hear there's a big storm coming from the west tonight."

"Thank you," she said as she started the car back up. "We will."

"Katherine?" June asked as they made their way back onto 11th Street. "We ain't eaten yet."

"Jesus, Mary, and Joseph, I completely forgot," said Kate. "I'm so sorry, June; you must be famished."

Kate didn't like to eat in the big cities because the cost was usually higher, so she took a left turn down Peoria Street in search of something reasonable. They decided to stop at Weber's Root Beer Stand in the Brookside area for a hamburger. As they sat down to look at the menu, June was trying to decide what to drink.

"June," said Kate as they took a seat at the counter. "The sign reads that this place is famous for their root beer. You should try it."

"I'm not sure I like root beer," June answered. "Only had it a couple of times when I was a kid."

"What about those wee root beer hard candies?" Kate asked as she put the menu down.

"The ones shaped like little barrels?" June answered. "Well, yeah, I like those."

"You should try the root beer is all I'm saying," Kate answered.

Just then a man sitting one seat from June broke in. "Begging your pardon, ma'am, but your friend is right."

Kate whispered to June, "Another truck driver."

The man continued. "Mister Bilby here makes the best root beer anywhere. Sez it's made with fourteen secret ingredients; makes it right here in his cellar."

Kate saw that familiar look in June's eyes whenever a man talked to her. June turned to him and asked, "So what are you saying?"

"Just that when you are at Weber's, you really should have the root beer," he answered. "They invented this recipe back in the 1880s."

"But what if I don't like it?" June said with a face that could melt butter.

"Tell you what, doll," he said. "I'll buy you the root beer, and then if you don't like it, there's nothing lost."

"But I don't even know your name," June answered.

"Holy cats!" He extended his hand. "The name's Jim Schuster, good to know you. Now how about that root beer?"

June looked at Kate for guidance.

"Mister Schuster here has made a genuine offer and solution to your dilemma. I think its best you make up your own mind on the matter." June could tell that Kate actually liked him.

Kate extended her hand to Jim. "I'm Mrs. Katherine Callahan. Happy to make your acquaintance."

June had to agree that not only was the root beer unlike any she had ever tasted but the cheeseburger was as well. She ate every last bite, including all her French-fried potatoes.

The conversation was pleasant as they ate. They told Jim about going to California and life in Chicago, and he regaled them with stories of life on the Mother Road and how six years ago he had even watched Hollywood do some filming of the movie *The Grapes of Wrath* through Oklahoma.

When they were finished and Kate was paying the tab, June and Jim went over toward the door. Kate turned just in time to see June hand him a piece of paper and plant a kiss on his cheek. He walked them to their car and opened the door for June.

"You ladies be careful out there," he said as he helped June into her seat. "Word is, there's a storm out west. Good to know you both, and you'll be hearing from me, June."

"Okay, Missy," Kate said the second they were back on the road, "and pray tell, what was that all about?"

"Oh, nothing really," answered June, her tone now changed when not talking to a man.

"Jim told me he goes through Illinois about twice a year. He asked if he could look me up. Oh, Katherine, men seem so different out here. Nothing like this ever happened to me in Chicago or Decatur. I really liked him."

"Well, I have to admit, I liked him, too," said Kate, smiling at June. "He was a nice enough man and a gentleman to boot. Remember, June, to always go with the gentlemen, not with every Tom, Dick, and Harry that might be turning your head with a wink."

"Were Wayne and John gentlemen?" June asked.

"Wayne was for certain. My husband was not as refined but was always a good caring man who would protect me to the end."

Kate fought back tears as she spoke. "I'm going to telephone John from our next stay. I'm going to tell him that I'm coming home to him and Sean-o--and to only them."

"You've made up your mind then, Katherine?" June said excitedly.

"Indeed I have," Kate answered. "How could I have been so stupid?"

After this, the ladies continued their journey happily through the state. As they bypassed Oklahoma City via Beltline 66, the sky began to grow dark. They became acutely aware that the men who had warned them about the approaching storm knew what they were talking about. By the time they reached Yukon, the rain was coming down hard. June switched on the radio and turned the dial. There was a good deal of static as she searched. She settled on KOMA, which had local news and weather. The announcer warned of flooding and washed-out bridges.

"Maybe we should stop," June finally said as the car started to sway from the wind.

"Yes, perhaps you're right. But I would like to keep going a wee bit more and see what we can find. Check the map. What town is coming up next?"

June read the map. "El Reno," she answered.

Once they reached the small town of El Reno, however, the rain looked like it had slowed down, so Kate decided to keep going. But as Murphy's Law would have it, the storm grew worse. The radio went to static for a moment and then came back, but what they heard made them feel strange. It was some sort of advertisement. They were speaking English, but the words made no sense: electronics emporium, IPod, 8-gig flash drive, digital camera with 14 mega-pixels. The background music was weird, too. Kate thought Oklahoma City must be an awfully strange place. She switched the radio off.

The storm grew wild around them as the ladies searched for a place to stop. They spotted a sign for Hinton and Bridgeport, and hoped either one would be a good choice.

June looked at the map and saw that Hinton was further south and neither town was directly on Highway 66. They watched as automobiles started to turn around and head back the other way. At this point, just up ahead, they could barely see what looked to be a lake. In reality, it was a bridge and the whole surface was covered with water. Kate mashed down hard on the brake pedal and the car skidded left and then right and finally onto the bridge. June screamed and grabbed onto Kate's sleeve. The car hit the bridge truss and stopped. The two women sat there for a second, hearts pounding in their chests.

The car was still running, so Kate wondered if they could make it across the bridge. June pleaded with her to reconsider. Just then another auto came swerving in a serpentine pattern onto the bridge, heading right for them. The ladies braced themselves in shocked silence as the car struck them in the rear. Their heads jerked back as Kate's car lunged forward and broke through the bridge rail. They almost went over, but the car stopped just in the nick of time. They turned to see the other car bounce off and barrel through the opposite guard, going over, down into the river.

Kate crossed herself. "Saints preserve us," she whispered. Then, getting angry, she yelled out, "Where are the authorities? Why haven't they put up roadblocks?"

"Come on, Katherine, we need to get off this bridge right now," June said in a shaky voice.

Kate made June get out of the car, and she slowly turned it around on the bridge and headed back off. At the bridge entrance, she pointed the headlamps toward any oncoming traffic and exited the car herself. Standing with June in the pouring rain, she said, "I'd rather lose my automobile then have someone else get hurt on this confounded bridge."

She tried looking over the edge where the car went over but saw nothing but blackness below.

"I'm going to try and climb down there," Kate said. "There might be folks needing our help."

"Katherine, are you crackers?" June yelled. "You can't go down there. It's pitch-black. You'll be killed."

Kate started to yell in an exasperated way. "I have to do something; we can't just let them die." She was pacing back and forth, still trying to see something down below. She stopped when she heard sirens and saw flashing lights as three police cars pulled up behind her Buick.

"Is everyone all right here?" one of the officers yelled as he got out of the car.

Kate frantically told him about the car that had crashed to the bottom. He assured the ladies that they would do everything they could.

"Is your car all right for driving?" one of the other men asked.

"I don't know," answered Kate. "We were hit in the back end." They looked the car over and saw that the rear fender was rubbing on the tire.

"Now, you listen to me," the first officer said. "I'm calling for a tow truck. You and your auto will be taken to Geary. The driver will help you find a nice warm place to stay for the night. I know the driver and he'll do everything he can to help you. He's also a good mechanic."

When the tow truck came, the two soaked ladies got in to stay warm. June was in complete awe of Kate. She had never experienced such bravery in a person, such selfless sacrifice. She wished she could be more like her. She knew that at that moment, Kate would have given up her life to try and save a complete stranger. She knew her own life was safe as long as she was with her new best friend, Katherine Callahan.

The driver hooked up Kate's Buick and got in. June saw right away that he was a handsome, rugged cowboy type. His hands showed signs of hard work. Just as the truck started to pull out, Kate thought she saw someone on the bridge. But when she blinked, the figure was gone.

The driver finally spoke: "Pleasure to make yer acquaintance," first looking at Kate, "Ma'am," and then to June, "Ma'am," tipping his cowboy hat each time. "The name's Taylor, but folks call me Sam. Had a bit of trouble at the old bridge eh? It's not the first time. The rain takes folks by surprise sometimes. Where you gals from?"

"We've come from Chicago," answered Kate, still shivering.

"Never been there, too big, too cold for my taste," Sam said. "You don't sound like you're from Chicago."

"Well, I was born in Ireland. My family came to Chicago when I was nineteen." Kate felt comfortable with Sam. It was nice to let go for a time and let someone else be the strong one.

82

"And what about you, pretty lady?" Sam asked, looking at June.

June immediately blushed. "I was born and raised in Chicago, and lived there until about two years ago. I still live in Illinois."

"Never even been to Illinois; never been east of Kansas," he answered. "This is where I was born and I reckon this is where I'll stay."

Sam booked them a room in the Jesse Chisholm Hotel. As he brought in their suitcases, he announced, "Now, you gals sleep sound. I'll have this here automobile running in tip-top shape by midmorning. They serve a nice breakfast here, so you just take yer time. Sun should be out tomorrow and the roads will be passable. You never said where you were going?"

June beat Kate to the punch in answering, "California."

"Never been there," Sam said. "Tomorrow I'll show you a shortcut back to the highway so's you don't have to backtrack. Anyway, the bridge will probably be closed for repairs. Night, now!"

Kate and June felt great getting into their clean, dry night wear. June was reflective as she lay in bed while Kate finished her night prayers. They had come close to being killed on that bridge, and they both felt how fragile their lives were. But right now in this moment, in this time, they felt safe and warm. Sleep came upon them quickly.

June woke up feeling refreshed. She saw Kate sitting up at the desk writing something. She got up and glanced over Kate's shoulder to see that it was a postcard.

"Good morning, June," Kate said, sounding bright and chipper.

"Morning," June answered, wiping sleep from her eyes.

"I went to the front desk to see if they had any cards from the hotel. They didn't carry them, but the lady gave me this one from Oklahoma. I'm a bit upset that I never got to phone John last night. By now he'll be at work. So I thought I'd write him."

"I couldn't help but notice you omitted a couple details from last night's adventure," June said.

"Oh?" Kate already knew what June was talking about.

June continued. "Yeah, like the fact that we were almost killed on that bridge."

Kate looked at her card. "I don't want John to worry any more than he has to. Now, get ready and let's go try their breakfast. We never had supper last night, and I'm starving."

Sam had been right, the breakfast was excellent. Kate had eggs sunny-side up, sausage, and fried potatoes. June had scrambled eggs, bacon, and toast. Both women had coffee. Kate thought the pork sausage was not like the bangers back in Ireland but still had a farm-fresh taste.

Just as they were leaving the hotel café, Sam met them outside. "Good morning, madams. See now, the rain is gone and there ain't a cloud in the sky. That's how it is in these parts. Your Buick is parked right around the corner, good as new. That'll be zero dollars and naught cents."

"Excuse me?" Kate asked.

"That's right," Sam chuckled. "The state pays for the tow and repairs in cases like this. Oh, and there's news about the other car that went over the bridge. A couple of young married folks in there. The filly is fine, which is a good thing cause she was in a family way. The young fella was taken to the hospital in Oklahoma City but is expected to be okay, too. Can't say as much for their automobile, though. It's beyond help. Miracle they weren't killed."

Kate crossed herself. "Thank God," she whispered.

Sam told them about an alternate route over the bridge and how to get back to the highway. June could follow it on her map. He shook both their hands as they said their good-byes and thanked him. It didn't take them long to work their way back to Highway 66 west of the river.

The next large town was Clinton where they stopped for gas, passing a place called Pop Hicks Restaurant. This made June think about her new hometown of Decatur since it had a similar coffee shop. That's when she realized that she was not homesick at all. She missed her parents but not her town. If they hadn't been so full from breakfast, she thought Pop Hicks would be a great place to stop for pie.

"Katherine," June started as they settled back into the drive, "I've been doing a lot of thinking about my life. I haven't been happy for such a long time. These past few days have been the happiest I can ever remember being."

"Perhaps you needed a vacation, June," said Kate.

"I needed a vacation from my whole life," June answered. "I've never had a good friend, even as a kid. You have become my very best friend. But besides that, I have to admit, it's the men I've met here. They're all so nice."

Kate smiled at June. "It helps that they're all rugged and a bit good-looking too, eh sweetie?"

"Well, yeah, that never hurts," June said.

They both laughed. When the silence ensued again, June continued, "I've been thinking about moving after our trip and settling down out here."

Kate looked surprised. "June, you've never lived alone in your entire life. You went from your dad and mum to your husband and then back to your dad and step mum."

"That's just it," June continued. "I ain't never taken a chance my whole life. I think it's time I grew up. I just love it out here. Back in Chicago, you know, it's still cold as hell. Here, it's warm, even in March. I bet I can find a nice house for cheap. I'm not rich, but Frank did leave me a little money."

"Well, it's a lovely thought, June," said Kate. "You'll do fine on your own, and you may even find yourself the perfect husband--eventually, that is. But don't be makin' up your mind just yet. We'll be in Texas soon, and you may find you like it there even better than Oklahoma."

At this thought, June smiled, half to Kate and half to herself.

As they reached Texola, June announced that they were nearing Texas. They marveled at the old pioneer feel of the wooden awnings and country stores. The wind had picked up, and they could feel the car sway as they approached the Oklahoma-Texas border. June felt a thrill knowing they would soon be in the West and among real cowboys and ranches. She remembered a line from *Gilda* uttered by Rita Hayward: *"If I'd been a ranch, they would've named me 'The Bar Nothing.'"* She wondered what it meant.

Then they saw it, a large stone sign welcoming them to Texas. The excitement welled up in June so much that she could take it no longer. Making a whirly motion in the air as if she were swinging an invisible hat or lasso, she yelled at the top of her lungs, "HEE HAW," scaring Kate half to death.

Kate felt lady luck could be with them when she saw the first town was called Shamrock. This had to be a good sign. She had hoped it would look like her old home of Ireland, but although it was a quaint nice town, it was all American. They noticed it was an oil town, and signs of money were evident. Kate was pleased to see that there were remnants of a St. Patrick's Day parade from a week or so earlier.

June marveled as they passed the art deco Tower Station and U-Drop Inn Restaurant. She thought this was the epitome of swank for such a small town. However, there was no reason to stop in Shamrock. They would soon be in the big city of Amarillo.

Entering the Texas plains, June had the impression that she was in a western movie. They also encountered large gullies in the road called washes, made over the years from the Texas Panhandle rains. But never was it more evident that they were in Texas than now, when Kate had to slam on her brakes yet once again, this time for a herd of cattle meandering on the road right after a sharp bend.

"Jesus, Mary, and Joseph," yelled Kate, feeling rather annoyed. "You just never know what you'll find along this highway."

June smiled, loving every minute of it. "How long do you suppose they'll stand here?" she asked Kate.

"And just how am I supposed to know a thing like that?" Kate snapped. "I can't get into a cow's head, now can I?"

Seeing Kate's frustration and Irish temper flaring up, June decided to put on her serious face. "Well, maybe we can sort of push them off the road."

"Oh, that's just splendid; we get out and risk our lives," Kate said, starting to turn three shades of crimson. "Can't you just see the newspapers in the morning: Two Chicago women lose their lives when they were trampled to death by a herd of cattle on U.S. 66."

June gave a laugh and exited the car. She circled around back so she could get behind the herd.

Kate rolled down her window and yelled, "June, what in God's name are you doing? Get back in the car this instant!"

But June ignored her. Once she was behind the cattle, she raised her arms in the air and in a real low, gravelly voice started talking to the animals. "Shoo now, cows, move along; shoo, you shoo now, Bessie."

Kate couldn't help but laugh, especially when she saw that the cattle were starting to move across the road. She thought that June looked a bit like Frankenstein's monster.

June kept going, "You move along now, little doggies; shoo now, git. I'm not playing a game with you; you move, you cows, you. Mooooove!"

When the last cow had crossed the road, June ran and got back in the car, Kate was laughing so hard, tears were coming down her face, but she managed to drive past the herd.

"Where did you learn to do that?" Kate asked.

"Gene Autry movies," June answered with a chuckle.

As they continued through the Texas plains, Kate fell solemn.

"Penny for your thoughts, dear," June said, looking at Kate over her glasses.

"Oh it's just that I don't know how long I can stand being away from my wee baby, my sweet Sean-o," Kate's voice cracked as she tried to hold back tears. "It's been over four days since I tucked him into his bed for the last time."

"From what you've told me," June answered, "John is a good father and the baby is also in good hands with your in-laws. I know you must miss him, but he'll be fine for two weeks. He was taking the bottle okay, wasn't he?"

Kate answered, "Yes, I never could have left if he weren't. My breasts are all but dried up now. Oh, dear God, why did I leave them? I miss them so much."

June looked out the window at a sign posting the Will Rogers Highway. "Call them--the next time we stop for gas. Or how about we stop in Amarillo for lunch, use the pay phone, and call. Why haven't you telephoned your mother-in-law?"

"They haven't got a phone," Kate answered, "and John will be at work."

"Tonight, then," June said. "Let's see, we should be in or near New Mexico. You can phone John tonight."

Kate smiled at June and added, "Sure, if we don't get stopped by another herd of cows."

* * * * *

Amarillo was a bright, clean city appearing out of the plains like Brigadoon. They passed a café they thought would be good, called the Blue Front Café, but it had a grand opening sign for a later date. So they stopped at another brand-new diner called the Golden Light Café, which specialized in hamburgers. June loved hamburgers, and although Kate found theirs to be delicious, she only ate half and urged June to do the same.

"Tonight for supper, I'd like to stop at a real restaurant," Kate told June. "I like the food at these roadside cafés and this hamburger is exceptional, but I've been longin' for a full, proper, sit-down meal."

"That would be swell, Katherine," said June. "Maybe we can find a good restaurant in New Mexico."

Before leaving, the man behind the counter warned them that if they were heading west, to make sure they bought gasoline in Texas since the gas tax was higher in the adjoining state.

As they left Amarillo, the sky began to turn gray and the wind picked up. It was becoming obvious that they were in for another storm. By the time they reached Adrian, the sky had grown so dark it appeared to Kate and June that it was the middle of the night. The wind pushed against the car, and lightning flashed all around them. They managed to drive though, but as the lights of the town vanished behind them, visibility became impossible. Kate saw what looked to be a roadside park and pulled in. June clicked on the radio and listened as the familiar hum turned to static. She finally found a news show from Amarillo that warned of a tornado approaching from the west.

"A tornado!" June cried out.

Kate patted June's hand. "It will be all right, sweetie. Let me move the car up behind that brick fireplace over there, and we'll stay put until it passes."

The wind became so fierce that June was sure the car would be turned over. Kate's mind went back to John's favorite movie and the twister that Dorothy encountered in *The Wizard of Oz*. Perhaps her car would be lifted up and taken to a magical place. She found herself saying out loud the famous phrase uttered by Judy Garland in the picture, "*There's no place like home.*" June looked at her and scowled, trying to figure out why she had said it.

Just when they thought it might be passing, the storm grew worse. The wind seemed to be whirling around them, and the lightning flashes were blinding. June grabbed Kate's arm. The radio went dead, and for a moment, they felt like they were standing still in time. Everything was dead quiet, and solid blackness engulfed the car.

Kate's thought went to the young man in her dream. It was like an extremely vivid apparition or vision. Although she had no idea who the man was, she felt a closeness to him in these few seconds.

Then came another lightning flash and a heavy lamppost came crashing down next to June's side of the car. She screamed and squeezed Kate's arm even harder.

Kate yelled out, "KEVIN!"

The storm was still around them but moments later had finally started to wane.

"Who's Kevin?" asked June when the imminent danger had passed.

"Pardon?" asked Kate.

"Kevin," June answered. "You called out the name Kevin."

"When?"

"Just now, when the lightning flashed," said June. "I screamed and you called out Kevin."

"I haven't the slightest idea," Kate answered while making sure the car was still running. "I was thinking about my dream from the other night and the man in church. Just now his face was in front of me. I've never seen him before, but there is something special about him."

"Well, maybe he's Kevin," June said. "Could be someone you knew a long time ago, or maybe you're being haunted."

"I don't think he's a ghost." Kate crossed herself just in case he was a poor soul in need of prayer. "I don't think he's anyone I knew from my past either, but perhaps he's someone I'll know in the future."

"Now you're talking queer. You some sort of Irish gypsy fortune teller?" June asked.

Kate laughed as she pulled back on the road. "By the way, June, you can let go of my arm now."

Looking on the map, June saw that they were about twenty miles from the New Mexico border. She reminded Kate to stop at a filling station in Glenrio and noticed that the town seemed to be in both Texas and New Mexico.

They stopped at the Phillips 66 on the Texas side and gassed up. June went inside to buy a new map for both New Mexico and Arizona. She noticed another customer who appeared to be even more out of place here among the cowboys than she was. He was a well-dressed man wearing a bowler. He noticed her staring at him and tipped his hat. As she was leaving the station, she noticed that the gentleman had a distinct accent as he talked to the attendant.

Getting back in the car, she told Kate about the man as they drove off. She said he sort of talked like Churchill. Kate glanced in her rearview mirror and could just barely see the man as he exited the station.

Chapter 8
Take the Highway That is Best

Clinton, Oklahoma
Present Day

Cheryl and I went back up to our respective rooms to get ready. We had decided to spend part of the day in Clinton to research the area, although I had to admit, my research consisted mostly of going to spots where my grandmother had been and feeling her presence. Cheryl had a more tangible approach.

Usually Cheryl would be knocking on my door first, but I finished early and went to her room. When she opened the door, I saw a distraught look on her face. She was reading from her Hebrew Scriptures. What I always found cool was the fact that she read them in the original Hebrew. I also noticed that she had the Gideon's, King James Bible from the room in front of her.

"What's the matter, sweetie, and what's with the Protestant Bible?" I asked.

"You know I sometimes like to compare passages in my Hebrew Bible with other translations," she answered.

"Okay, so what were you reading and how did the Christian Bible stack up?" I asked.

She paused for a second before answering. "I was reading the story of how Esther saved the Jewish people from extermination in Persia by the hand of the king's adviser, Haman. Esther was young, Jewish, and beautiful, and . . ."

"Like you," I interrupted.

"Yeah, right. Anyway, to make a long story short," she continued, "she talked the king into saving the Jewish people. The King James was faithful to the translations I'm used to. It's just nice to read a story in a slightly different way than how I've read it since childhood."

"So, I still don't get it--what's wrong?" I asked.

"Like all good Jewish holidays," she answered, "this story is to be celebrated forever and we do. It's called Purim."

"Oh, yeah, I remember that one. Sort of the Jewish Mardi Gras," I answered, trying to lighten up the mood.

"That's right, that's what you always called it. Kevin, today is the fourteenth day of Adar. Today is the first day of Purim. It started at sundown last night. I miss my family. If I were home, I'd be with David and my parents. I should be celebrating and also I should have gone to temple on Saturday. I'm sure I could have found one in Missouri, like you found a Catholic church on Sunday."

Does travel excuse attendance?" I asked.

"You don't get it," she scolded. "It's not like we HAVE to go to Synagogue on Saturdays. We go because we want to go, to honor G-d and keep his commandments."

I put my arm around her shoulder. "How about this? We stay here instead of driving on tonight and do our own celebrating. It may not be traditional food and fare, but we can still make the best of it. We can even put our research on hold for the day. What do you say?"

"Kevin, you are a great friend," she said, touching my hand. "I almost forgot that when I'm with you, I *am* with family. I will take you up on your offer. But I still want to continue our research as long as we're here."

"Cool!" I said.

"Hey," she yelled before I could walk out the door. "We can't drive anyway. This is the one day of the year that the Talmud says we must drink enough to blot out the name of Haman."

"You mean you're required to drink?" I asked.

"Yes, indeed, it's an actual mitzvah," she answered. "We are to drink enough to get so sloshed that we can't discern between the name of Purim's hero Mordechai and the villain Haman. It humbles us so we can appreciate that only G-d can truly discern between good and evil."

"I love it, a religion that requires you to drink on a feast day. Well, come to think of it, I bet if I were to ask old Father O'Malley, I might get the same answer," I joked. "Anyway, that's cool. Besides, I want to talk to that old guy again tonight. What was his name?"

"Sam Taylor," she answered and kissed me on the cheek.

"Call your parents," I suggested.

"Yes, I will, and David, too," she said.

I really had no reason to, but I found myself flinching at the sound of his name.

After breakfast, Cheryl took the car, and on her return, she handed me a bag. She told me how they were required to give the gift of food today. Only she couldn't find a Jewish bakery or anyone who made Hamentaschen.

"You mean those fruit-filled pastries that are shaped like a three-sided hat?" I asked.

"Those are the ones," she answered. "So I found the Polish version, kolachki, and also triangular shaped cookies that resemble them. We can eat them later."

"Nuh-uh," I said as I grabbed one of each.

I dropped Cheryl off in town so she could do her thing and decided to drive around and backtrack to the spot we had passed in the storm. Sure enough, just as Sam and the Internet had said, the place where we parked last night was abandoned. Just a small rest area and a gutted out café were all that remained--not the beautiful roadside park Cheryl and I had sat in. I wondered if the storm had played with our perceptions.

I drove back a bit more and came to the Pony Truss Bridge. Just like before, I got that sinking feeling and the emotion of great fear. I know Grandma Kate was at this bridge and very distressed. I parked and got out of the car. Walking a ways onto the bridge, I stood there for the longest time, my eyes going between the picture in Grandpa John's pocket watch and the water down below.

Then something strange happened. The water started to entrance me. I felt as if it were a conduit straight to Grandma Kate--or more accurately, to the past. As I stared at the water down below with only the thoughts of my grandmother in my head, I felt like night had engulfed me. I heard the sound of brakes squealing and cars crashing. I looked to my right and saw an old-time car turn around and park in front of the bridge entrance. I heard the sound of sirens and saw police lights. It was then that I saw a woman who looked like Grandma Kate along with another woman get into a vehicle, like a tow truck. I started to run and call out, but as soon as I reached the edge of the bridge, it all faded and there I was on this quiet road at midmorning.

Was I seeing what really happened that night, or was it just my overactive imagination? I didn't have a map, since Cheryl and her 4G served that purpose, so I just followed my instincts and started driving up Route 8. I felt the familiar feeling of being on the very path that my grandmother had traveled until I found myself in Geary. I knew instinctively that this was where she stayed. Hadn't Sam Taylor said that he drove a tow truck from Geary? Yes, I needed to talk to that man tonight. Eventually, I lost her scent, so to speak, and had to head back to the interstate the way I came.

I met back up with Cheryl, who was sitting in the motel lobby drinking a Coke and looking through her smartphone. I told her all about my experience on the bridge and asked her who she supposed the other woman was with Grandma Kate.

"Perhaps she was another driver involved in the accident," she surmised. "You did say you heard the sound of a crash?"

"Yes," I answered, "but it was all dreamlike, and I wasn't sure what I saw and heard. There was only the one car along with the police and the tow truck. How about you, Cher? Did you find anything?"

"Well, not so much from this area," she answered. "I confirmed that there was a storm here on March 24, 1946, and the Pony Truss Bridge was closed for repairs. But I made another big discovery from the feelers I sent out, and I mean *big*."

"Come on, Cher, spill it," I said, taking a sip from her pop.

She looked at me reluctantly. "I discovered that one Wayne Peterham booked a room at the Alvarado Hotel in Albuquerque on March 25, 1946."

"I KNEW IT!" I yelled.

"Now, let's not jump the gun here," she said quickly. "It might not even be him."

"Yeah, sure, because Peterham is such a common name, right? Cheryl, what was the next postcard from my grandmother?"

"Now, Kevin, listen . . ."

"Where was it from?" I interrupted angrily.

"Here it is, and yes, it was from the Alvarado, but . . ." She held up the card.

"So, tell me, did you find a Katherine Callahan booked there?" I asked.

"Well, no."

"That's because she was with him," I stammered.

"We don't know that, Kevin. Let's not jump to conclusions without definite confirmation. I know it looks bad, but if we are to believe what Grandma Kate told you in that dream that things were not as they seemed. Reading what she wrote in this card to Grandpa John, it just doesn't fit. And remember, the stamp *is* upside down."

"Let me see that card," I said, trying to hold back my anger.

THE FRED HARVEY ALVARADO HOTEL
ALBUQUERQUE, NEW MEXICO

Dearest John,

I wish you were here with us to see this beautiful city. There is a great Spanish mix with American culture here. I long to hold you once again in my arms, darling, and Sean-o, too. Give him a kiss from his mummy. I love you, John.

Yours truly,
Kate

I had to be alone with my thoughts. I was never more confused by anything in my life. I felt bad that I snapped at Cheryl; I wasn't angry with her. I was just hurt by the thought of my grandma possibly having had an affair that led to her disappearance. If she was in Albuquerque with this Wayne guy, how could she be so cavalier in writing about "us" to Grandpa John? I went up to my room to lie down. There were so many images in my head: Grandma Kate on the bridge, the pocket watch, the strange lady with her, Wayne Peterham, and the Alvarado Hotel. The thoughts whirled around until they all zeroed in on one single image--my Grandma Kate. There she was again, right in front of me, smiling. She was radiant and beautiful. She spoke quietly and dreamlike. "Things are not as they seem, Kevin. Follow me."

I crossed myself. "Grandma Kate," I begged, "please tell me what happened to you."

"Follow me to the truth," she said. "It will be difficult to hear, me boy. Be strong. Things are not as they seem. Follow me. Come and save me."

I woke up with jerk. I looked around the room because my grandmother's presence felt so real. As the reality set in that this was yet another dream, I felt calmness sweep over me.

At that moment, I knew beyond a shadow of a doubt that I was doing the right thing and that I would eventually find out what had eluded my family for so many years. I was glad to have the darkness lift from me.

In the meantime, I had to fix things with Cheryl. I had to be there to celebrate with her like I promised. I grabbed the bag of cookies, and after brushing my teeth, I headed for Cheryl's room. It was not yet sundown, so we still had time to start our holiday on the first day of Purim.

We had decided on a joint called the Turf Club. It was suppose to be a higher-end bar and grill. It was labeled as a great date spot on the Internet. As we settled in and ordered our first drinks of the night, I briefed Cheryl about my dream.

"But what in the world could she have meant by 'come and save me'?" she asked.

"I don't know, but I feel we're on a very important mission somehow. "Every time I have one of these dreams, I feel stronger about what we're doing."

"But how can you save her and from what?" she asked.

"Not sure," I answered. "Maybe it's to save her reputation, but I'm confident we'll find out--with your special help, of course."

"I'm here for ya, dude," she said in between ordering a steak and a bottle of Moet White Star.

Like me, Cheryl was not a big drinker, but the stress of missing her family on the holiday and my outburst must have made her feel like she really needed it, because she drank more and faster than I've ever seen her do, even on Purim--although she would just say it was the mitzvah. I started to get worried but then thought it might be best to allow her to let her hair down. She ordered another bottle of Moet.

I decided to temper my own alcohol intake so I could watch her. Besides, I was driving.

"Kevie, you are the bestest friend in the world." She clinked my glass with hers.

"I try, Cher. You aren't so bad yourself," I said.

"Ha," she slurred. "Who else would celebrate with me out here in the middle of nowhere?"

"Well, we're not exactly in the middle of nowhere," I corrected. "Clinton is actually a pretty nice metropolitan city."

"Yeah, you're right. I just love you," she said.

"I love you too, Cher."

"Nope, you don't. Hey, Kev, why is there so much bad in the world?"

"Like what?" I asked.

She looked sad as she answered. "We just passed Oklahoma City; I can't even hear the name without thinking about the bombing. Then there's 911, and soon we'll be in Texas where that horrible Fort Hood shooting happened. My Bubbe Adi was imprisoned by Nazis, your Grandma Kate disappeared, and your dad was raised without a mommy. I love the world, but why is it so awful sometimes?"

"I don't know, sweetie," I answered. "But I love the world too, and for all the bad, there is a thousand times more goodness here. Besides, this is supposed to be a celebration."

"I love you, Kevie," she said as her head dropped slightly.

"I love you too, Cher."

"No, you don't, but you're right, let's dance."

I grabbed her hand and led her up to the dance floor where they were playing some lively country song I had never heard before, and we danced the night away.

I had switched to Coke right after I ate and drove carefully back to the hotel. I helped Cheryl into her room and into bed. I thought to myself that she was going to feel this in the morning. As I pulled the covers up around her, she tried to kiss me but I pulled away. When she sank back onto her pillow, I bent down and kissed her on the forehead. After securing her door, I went down to the front desk to talk to Sam Taylor.

Sam was there, just like the night before. "How you doing this fine evening, young fella? Hey, weren't you with a pretty filly last night?"

"Ah yes, my friend, Cheryl." I answered.

"I thought so. I never forget a pretty face. But then again, I remembered you." Sam chucked to himself. "What can I do for ya? Room okay?"

"The room is fine," I answered. "Actually I'm hoping you can remember a pretty face who may have crossed your path once."

Sam grinned. "Like I said, I never forget a pretty face. I always had a hankerin' for the ladies. Never settled down, mind you, but I do enjoy the company of the fairer sex. So when might I have crossed paths with this one: last month, last year?"

"Well, actually over sixty years ago," I answered.

"What in the devil? Look here, young fella. I've got a good memory, but do you have any idea how many ladies I've met in the past sixty years?"

"I know it's a long shot, and maybe you never even met her," I continued. "But I am searching for my grandmother who went missing along Route 66 back in 1946. We know from a postcard that she was in this area and may have had some trouble at the Pony Truss Bridge. I have reason to believe she had her car towed."

Sam looked thoughtful. "During storms, that bridge gave many a person a hard time back then. Well, if she had her car towed from the bridge, I would have been the one doing the towin'. I was the only driver in the area. Had my own tow truck; used it till about 1963."

I interrupted his banter and showed him the picture of Grandma Kate from the pocket watch. He looked at it intently. I could see he was going through the drawers of many files in his brain.

"June," he finally said.

"No, it would have been March," I corrected.

"No, sonny, the name 'June' comes to my mind. At the time, I'd never heard a woman called by a month, except for Mae, but that's spelled differently."

My face dropped as low as my spirits because now I was thinking that old Sam was maybe a bit senile.

He spoke again, very slowly, his thoughts trying to capture the moment. "Wait, June was her friend; this one's name was . . . Katherine, I think. Spoke with an Irish accent." At this, the bounce came back to his speech. "Yes siree, I do remember this one. One of the most beautiful women I've ever had the pleasure to meet, had the bluest eyes. That was your grandmother?"

"Please, Sam, tell me all you can remember about her. You said her friend's name was June?" I asked.

"That's right, June," he answered. "She was a bit more plain than Katherine but still pretty and very nice. They both treated me with respect. I could tell they were city folk, and often people like that treated us like country bumpkins or something. Not these two. But then again, they had gone through a rough night. Had an accident on the old bridge. They saw another car go off and crash down below. Officer Crump said that your grandmother was particularly worried and even wanted to climb down and save the people herself. Had a lot of spunk, that one. Now it's all starting to come back to me. Drove them to Geary for the night and fixed up their car. Said they were headin' for California. Never been there myself. That was about it."

"Where did they stay in Geary?" I asked.

"A place called the Jesse Chisholm Hotel," he answered. "Not there anymore. Too bad too, it was a nice place."

"Would there be any records? Do you remember June's last name?" I asked.

"Nope, never remember last names, just first and only the ladies." Sam made me laugh--ninety something and still a lady's man.

"Hold on there, young fella. There is someone who might be able to help you with that. The Chisholm often made it a policy to write down the names of all the guests, not just the one who registered. I have a lady friend who lives just a few blocks away who has those records. She was the hotel manager back in the late 1950s when the place closed. She kept the register books, not sure why. You want me to give her a call?"

"Isn't it too late?" I asked.

"Nonsense," he said, grabbing a pad of paper. "She's always held a bit of a torch for yours truly. I'll give her a call and maybe have the information to you by morning. I won't be here, but I'll leave it for you. Now, what's that exact date?"

"That would be March 24, 1946," I answered. "Thank you so much, Sam. It was a pleasure meeting you."

"Likewise," he said. "And give my regards to that filly of yours."

* * * * *

"Did you tell him I'm not your filly?" Cheryl asked as I related the whole story to her the next morning. "Oh, my aching head. Why did you let me drink that much?"

"To blot out the memory of Haman, of course," I said with a grin.

"Well, it worked. I don't remember a thing," she said, holding her head.

I was glad she didn't remember trying to kiss me when I tucked her in last night. I wondered if that memory would return to her.

I waited for Cheryl to get ready before going down to the desk to see if Sam had left the info. Cheryl made a beeline right to the coffee.

When I asked, the girl behind the desk looked in my slot and handed me a hand-printed letter.

To Kevin Callahan,

*** This is all my friend could dig up. I hope you find what you're looking for.***

Registered: Katherine Callahan

License Plate: Illinois, 1357
Residence: Chicago, Illinois

Second Occupant: June Franklin
Residence: Decatur, Illinois

Good Luck,
Sam

"Cheryl," I said, handing her the note, "have we heard this name before?"

She looked at it. "Of course. If I didn't have this wicked hangover, it would have registered the minute you said the name June. Oy vey, Kevin, don't you remember? It's the woman Mrs. Majewski told us about--the one Grandma Kate got in trouble with for fighting."

"Oy vey is right!" I said. "But didn't Mrs. Majewski say she was a nasty woman and treated my grandmother horribly?"

"Yeah, she did," Cheryl answered.

"But Sam said she was nice," I stated.

"Well, sometimes people change," she said. "So, you see, her companion wasn't Wayne Peterham after all."

"That still doesn't explain the fact that he was registered at that Albuquerque hotel on that date," I answered.

Cheryl's head was starting to clear from her coffee elixir. "That reminds me, I have to make a call. Hey, Kev, you did good."

"Thanks, kiddo. Maybe I should consider a career change," I said.

"Ah, let's not jump the gun here, brainiac." She grinned.

After eating breakfast and checking out, Cheryl started to feel even better. It was good to get back on the road, even if Historic Route 66 was directly under the interstate at this point. We didn't bother going on Business 40 through Elk City, but just past Sayre we found a good, long stretch of the old road that went through Erick and then on through Texola. Once past the border, I couldn't believe we were already in Texas. True to herself, Cheryl broke out into a chorus of "Deep in the Heart of Texas," Pee Wee Herman–style. I joined in at the clapping part and made a joke about finding Grandma Kate in the basement of the Alamo. I sensed a concentration of my grandmother when we passed Shamrock, but I felt it didn't hold any real importance. We had to endure a long stretch of interstate but were excited to finally reach Amarillo.

Cheryl got the answer to her phone call. She discovered that along with Wayne Peterham being registered at the Alvarado, June Franklin was also registered there that same night. She informed me that this was why we couldn't find Grandma Kate there--they had registered under June's name.

I was impressed with Cheryl's ability but also her steadfast need for the facts before jumping to conclusions. I needed to work on that, especially since my grandmother kept telling me in dreams that things were not what they seemed.

"Cheryl, what do you suppose my dreams are all about?" I asked.

"What do you mean?" she asked, nose still in her laptop.

I continued, "I mean, who is sending them to me? Is it a ghost or a saint from heaven or some sort of energy imprint of my late grandmother?"

"Who said anything about LATE?" she asked. "We don't know for sure that she ever died."

"Yeah, there I go again," I said. "But she looks young and beautiful like she did back then."

"I don't know," she said. "This one is beyond my ability. But okay, for the sake of argument, let's say she had died. What do Christians believe?"

I answered, "Well, most believe that the soul leaves the body and goes to one of two places. The wicked go to eternal damnation or hell. Personally I believe one would have to completely and with full knowledge sever themselves from the love of God to be sent there. The righteous go to heaven to be with God. We Catholics call these saved souls the Communion of Saints. But for us, there is a third place that is also part of this communion. It's for the souls who die with unreconciled sins. They are saved and will eventually be with God in heaven, but they first go to a temporal place of purification called Purgatory. It's like you can steal a car and be sorry and even be forgiven, but you still have to return the car or pay for it."

"Well, Kev," she started, "while Jews have similar beliefs, we are not so cut and dry with them. In other words, the Talmud allows us to have many beliefs and many options. One of these beliefs is that a soul is first born in heaven. In the mother's womb, he or she is given full knowledge of life in accordance with the Talmud but right before birth is touched by an angel and all is forgotten. The angel puts his finger on the baby's lips and says, '*Shhhh.*' Legend has it that this is why we have an indentation on our upper lip. He or she is then born into this world with a mission for life. When we die, our soul has full knowledge again. We can be with G-d or go to a place similar to your purgatory or to hell, but some believe that the wicked soul just ceases to exist. But the main point is the mission. We are all given a mission, and Jews believe by some mystics that if we don't accomplish our mission, we can come back. This concept is called *Gilgul Neshamot,* which is really just reincarnation. But who's to say the mission can't be accomplished through others."

"Hmmm," I said. I had to give this some thought. "I certainly don't believe in reincarnation. Here's a question for you. Why would a soul be given full knowledge in the womb just to have it taken away before birth?"

"That, my friend," she answered, "is the classic paradox rabbis have struggled with for centuries. If you think about it, your belief in a G-d that has the Father the same as the Son is a huge paradox also. Both our faiths have unanswered mysteries."

I put my hand around her shoulder and petted her soft hair. "I'm so glad to have you as my best friend," I said. She gave me a quirky little half smile and went back to her laptop.

I was getting hungry and also felt that familiar close vibe to my grandmother as we drove down Amarillo's 6th Avenue. This was the old Route 66 through town. The feelings got stronger and stronger as I drove--I likened it to Marvel's Spider-Man and his spider senses--until I zeroed in on the site and found a parking spot. We went in the Golden Light Café, and I just knew that Grandma Kate had been in here, no doubt along with June Franklin. We feasted on their great burgers in a true Route 66 landmark location. It was nice and rare that there was still a place along the route that existed from 1946.

Parallel Roads (Lost on Route 66)

Leaving Amarillo, I felt good as we passed the Cadillac Ranch with its famous line of dead cars from different eras. I knew this monument didn't exist in Grandma Kate's time, but it was still great to see the Historic Route 66 exhibit.

As we drove west on I-40, the sky became dark with clouds. Cheryl confirmed that a huge storm was approaching us head-on. She said it made the last storm look like a spring drizzle. I thought it would be best to stop for gas in the next town and also a jug of water, since we were heading for the arid states. That town was Vega. Looking at it on the map, it was so typical of towns along Route 66. You could see where Business 40, which was old Route 66, went right through town while the main interstate swooped below, bypassing all of it. I knew there were many businesses taken out when this happened all along 66. Cheryl read that in towns like Vega there used to be facilities called lockers, which were large commercial freezers. People in the old days didn't have home freezers and would utilize these lockers. They would also sell to travelers out of them. Now they were just part of the ghosts from the past.

I paid for the gas and a five-gallon container of water using cash. I couldn't believe there were still places in America that wouldn't accept credit cards. He apologized and handed me my change, mostly in singles. The man was sputtering about heading west and some ghost town named Glenrio on the border of New Mexico, but I was only half listening.

I headed back to the car. "Can you believe places like this still exist?" I asked as I put the water in the back. I looked at Cheryl's face, which was ashen. "What is it?" She looked straight ahead like she was gathering her thoughts or afraid to speak. I noticed a tear running down her cheek. "Cheryl, what is it sweetie?"

With a shaky voice, she finally spoke. "I can't be a hundred percent sure, but I have this sinking feeling that the news article I just received in my e-mail is about Grandma Kate and June. It's not good news, Kevin."

"Tell me," I urged.

"It's from Kingman, Arizona, and dated March 28, 1946. It says that the bodies of two unidentified women were discovered in the desert along Route 95. It appears that the partially naked women were brutally beaten and left to die." She paused before going on, trying to hold back the tears. "It states that they were white and believed to be in their early thirties. No forms of identification or belongings were found on or near the bodies. It says, 'Further investigations by Arizona Police are pending.' Oh, Kevin!" She threw her arms around my neck.

I sat there holding Cheryl as she sobbed with tears running down my own cheeks. I was completely stunned. Maybe it wasn't them. Maybe they were raped. Maybe Wayne murdered them. I should have given up right then and there, but instead I found new determination. I was pissed and was going to find her murderer. I was going to find my Grandma Kate. I kissed Cheryl on the cheek, started the car, and peeled out, heading right for the storm.

Cheryl made a couple of phone calls before the weather could interfere with the reception. She called the colleague who sent her the news article. She called David and then talked to her mom. It seemed in every aspect that this trip had taken a different turn. I didn't know what was up ahead, but I knew there was something important.

The storm grew fierce as we passed the midpoint water tower and café by the same name in Adrian. Before hearing the news, it would have been fun knowing we were halfway from Chicago to Santa Monica on Route 66, but not this day.

Just west of town, it was getting horrific, and Cheryl informed me that a tornado had been spotted in the area. I didn't need her mobile Internet to inform me of that, though. There it was, just to the right of us. I pulled off the road and parked under the bridge at County Road 22. I tried to pull the car up under the bridge and not on the road itself. The winds were incredible. I don't know why, but I instinctively grabbed Grandpa John's pocket watch, as it comforted me somehow.

As the twister got closer, the sound was like that of a huge freight train going by. Cheryl grabbed hold of my shoulder and pressed her head deep into my chest. The sky was black as night and the rain pounded, but I had no fear, just dead calm and determination. I stared at the rain on the windshield until I was almost in a trance. Just then, lightning struck, and I swear it must have actually hit my car. Cheryl screamed, but as the sound of her yell faded, so did all the sights and sounds around us. We were sitting there in dead silence and blackness, a strange vibration all over our bodies. Cheryl and I looked at each other with just the dashboard lights to illuminate our faces. We wondered if we were in the eye of the storm.

The calm silence seemed to last for minutes, but in reality it was probably only a few seconds. Then another lightning strike hit. This time, it was *me* who yelled out. We were back in the storm but we saw the strangest thing. The bridge we were under was gone. We were sitting next to a field on the side of the road. Did the tornado move us miles away without us feeling anything? Cheryl tried her 4G, but as expected it was dead and so were our phones.

"Um, Kevin?" she asked, tapping me on the shoulder. "What happened to the bridge?"

"I haven't the slightest idea," I said, straining to look behind us. "I'll try the radio."

There was nothing but static on FM, so I switched to AM. Just like in the storm back near Clinton, I heard old-time radio broadcasts.

Cheryl was getting frustrated, still trying to get her 4G signal. "Oy, they really like broadcasting this old stuff out here, don't they?"

I finally found some local news that talked of the twister, but then the next few stories made Cheryl and I stop dead again. They were delivered in quick secession:

"In Washington, President Truman cooperated closely with the Republican leaders on foreign policy but fought them on domestic issues."

"A new eye-popping two-piece bathing suit called a bikini was unveiled in Paris this week."

"Winston Churchill coined a new phrase from his speech delivered March 5 on the spread of Communism in the Soviet Union. He referred to it as the Iron Curtain."

"A new Irving Berlin musical about Annie Oakley is set to open at Broadway's Imperial Theater in New York City sometime this spring called *Annie Get Your Gun*."

"With GIs returning from the war, people are trying to buy new cars with little success, as many of the factories have not yet been converted back to produce automobiles. People can expect to pay twenty five percent more than last year."

"What the hell is going on here?" I said, hitting the radio's power button to off. It had just occurred to me that throughout the whole storm and the unexplained removal of us or the bridge, the car had remained running. The winds had died and the storm turned into a steady rain. I pulled back onto the road and noticed another oddity. We were no longer on I-40, and unlike the usual Historic Route 66 signs, there was an old-style black-and-white Texas U.S. 66 signpost and another with the words "The Will Rodgers Highway."

"We *must* have been picked up and moved," I said. "We're back on Route 66 somehow."

"If only my computer would connect, I could tell us," she answered. "But I thought the old route along here was *under* the interstate. That is, if we're still near Adrian."

Chapter 9
Gallup through New Mexico

Chicago
March 25, 1946

John left work as usual Monday evening. It had been a rough weekend and a rough day on the job. He had been so worried about Kate and about taking care of Sean. Before picking up the baby from his parents' apartment, he wanted to stop for some groceries. He brought along the little booklet that the hospital had given to Kate. In it was a recipe for formula. He had to buy Carnation milk and dark Karo syrup. The boiled water, he could do.

He stopped at the A & P grocers on Kedzie Avenue where he ran into Lidia Majewski. He recognized her from a Bruning Christmas party that he and Kate attended, but had forgotten how tall she was. He liked her prominent Polish accent.

"John Callahan," she announced as she saw him in the cereal aisle. "How are you? We were wondering how Katherine was after the baby came."

John looked down into her cart and saw among other items a white paper wrapped package of ground pork, milk, Wonder bread, a box of Cheerioats, and one bag of Eight O'Clock Coffee.

"My dear wife has taken a trip to California to see her sister," he answered.

She looked at him knowingly. "Well, I didn't want to pry, but I did receive a postcard and I wondered what was going on. Is she alright?"

"She'll be home soon," he answered. "She just needed to get away for a spell. I now have to figure out how to make this formula for Sean."

"I hear they make one in a can now," Lidia announced. "It's supposed to be better for babies because it has more vitamins. You might want to look for it. Well, it was nice seeing you, John. Give my warmest regards to Katherine when you hear from her. God bless"

"I will, Lidia," he said, reaching for her outstretched hand. "Thanks for being a good friend to her while I was abroad."

She nodded a smile and walked on toward the cashier.

John didn't feel much like chatting at his parents' house, so he picked up Sean and went straight home to the empty apartment. Oh, how he missed Kate. He was almost grief stricken with worry, a melancholy woman out there on the road by herself. What if something happened to her? What if she never came back? How would he raise their son alone? He looked through the day's mail and found a postcard she had sent from Springfield, Illinois.

"Oh, Kate," he yelled to the walls. "Be safe and come home soon." He made the Sign of the Cross and recited the Our Father.

Once he was sure the baby was asleep, he squished a bag of Oleo with his hands to mix the yellow color into the white glob and put it in the ice box. He then made himself a quick sandwich for supper and grabbed a jacket. He decided to sit outside since the cold spell had finally broken. His thoughts were of his beautiful wife. How he missed the way life once was. But he believed in his heart that once she got back, they would be happy again. He listened for the baby and thought for a moment that he had heard the telephone ringing at the end of their long hallway.

New Mexico
March 25, 1946

The road narrowed and became bumpier as soon Kate and June crossed the state line at Glenrio. But unlike the Texas part of town, this side had shops and other businesses. Kate was still wondering who the stranger might have been whom June saw at the filling station. She had also caught a glimpse of the man dressed in black with a bowler. She naturally thought of Wayne but dismissed it quickly, as she had never known him to wear a hat.

As they drove, June was thinking about the nice men she had met in Oklahoma. The truck driver, Rocky, had looked at her like she was Dorothy Lamour. She had never been looked at by a man that way and she would never forget it. She also thought about Jim Schuster who bought her the root beer. She had hopes that he would make use of her phone number and address when she got back home. And even Sam Taylor was as nice a man as anyone could meet. She thought that maybe Texas didn't have this sort of man, at least not one they had met, and wondered if New Mexico might be different. She was still thinking hard about moving to Oklahoma.

Kate was deep in thought as well. She was thinking how she would find a nice place in Albuquerque to sit down and telephone John. She longed to hear his voice and regretted that she had been so distant with him the last time they saw each other. Wayne was starting to become a distant memory: one she would always cherish in the recesses of her heart, but one that would remain locked away there for the rest of her days.

They had left the storm far behind and were taken by the beauty of the New Mexico landscape. The sun was out and the sky was a cobalt blue. Never had either lady witnessed a sky like this. It literally took their breath away.

"That's just the cat's meow, huh, Katherine?" commented June. "Hey, do you think we can stop for a soda or something? I'm getting thirsty."

"Sure, sweetie," said Kate. "I'm feeling a wee bit parched myself. What's the next town, then?"

"Let's see," June looked down at her map. "We just passed Bard, so we should be getting to San Jon real soon."

In the few miles between Bard and San Jon, Kate couldn't shake the feeling that there was a presence around her, following her. Was it the dry air or the color of the sky? Was this what she had read back in Ireland as a child, about how the American Indians felt out in the Wild West? The land was sacred, and even though it wasn't part of her Christian beliefs, she felt akin to the idea of being on a spiritual quest. She couldn't put her finger on this feeling but felt there was something in the air. She pulled the car off the road and got out, leaving June to wonder why. She looked at the road behind them with the dark clouds in the distance.

June joined her. "What is it, Katherine?"

"I'm not sure," Kate answered. "I'm right here with you, in the here and now, but it's like I'm being followed by both my past and my future. It's as though, if I just waited here long enough, I'd be meetin' up with both"

"What are you talking about?" asked June, pushing up her glasses.

Kate smiled at her. "Oh, I know it must sound queer to you, and I'm sorry for that. I don't understand it myself. It's similar to how you feel about your future being out here somewhere, maybe Oklahoma, but your past is in Chicago. I feel my future is behind me too but approaching along with the past. Oh, never mind. The more I try and explain it, the more confused I feel."

What she did next also could not be explained, even to herself. She took a twenty-dollar bill from her handbag, and holding it up in the breeze for a second or two, she let it go. Maybe she was making an offering to the land around her or making some sort of restitution for leaving the way she did. Perhaps it was even a donation to the universe for a glimpse of her future. She had no idea, just a strong feeling that this was what she needed to do. Perhaps some down-and-out person or a family with a child would find it, someone who needed it. As she let it go, she heard a small yelp come from June, who then decided not to mention it.

San Jon was a real cowboy town. They stopped at a Gulf station and bought four ice-cold Pepsi-Colas and a bag of Spanish peanuts. As usual, June took notice of the men and found the Mexican gentlemen who worked the store, kind and courteous. One had soft brown eyes that sort of made her melt when he looked at her. Kate had taken notice of the red chili peppers that hung in bunches outside to dry and got a nice feeling from seeing them.

Back on the road, Kate and June did not stop again until Santa Rosa, only gazing as they passed historical markers such as the Comanche Trail, Tucumcari Mountain, Coronado's Route, the Goodnight Trail and the Trail of the 49ers. June felt an exhilaration knowing that they were in the midst of so much history.

They stopped at a Sinclair filling station, this time for gasoline and another drink. By now, the sun was setting low in the sky, which made the colors amazing. Santa Rosa consisted mostly of Mexican people who were warm and welcoming. As Kate paid for the gas and drinks, she noticed a car pull up and the man with the bowler exit from within. She strained to see through the glass window as he talked to the station attendant. June joined her after using the lavatory. As they left the station, Kate met the man eye to eye. She gasped as the shock of recognition set in.

"Hello, Katherine," he said.

"Wayne!" Kate yelped.

"What?" asked June.

"June, I would like you to meet Wayne Peterham."

"The pleasure is mine," he said. But June just looked at Kate.

"Wayne, what in God's green earth are you doing here?" Kate asked bitterly.

"I couldn't let you just walk out of my life," he answered. "I tried following you. I got on this highway and kept driving. I had stopped up in Santa Fe when I figured I was just wasting my time, so I turned back. Then I saw your automobile pull away back there in Texas. It was then I realized that I must have been driving ahead of you all this time. But my auto broke down and I lost precious time getting it repaired."

"Oh, Wayne," Kate said. "You shouldn't have come. Just when I was starting to pull my life back together."

"Katherine, you have to give me one more chance," he answered. "You *have* left your husband, have you not?"

"No, I . . ." Kate started to cry.

Wayne started to put his arm around Kate but June pushed it away and positioned herself between them. She put her own arm around Kate instead.

"All right," said Wayne. "Let's not talk here. Let me buy you dinner and you can just hear me out."

Kate scowled at him intently, "Are you out of your mind, Wayne? We have talked all we're going to. It was settled back in Chicago. I said my good-bye and that was it. The fact that you would get in your car and follow me across six states is quite unsettling."

"Creepy actually," said June.

Wayne looked forlorn. "I'm so sorry, my dear. I was just so desperate. I sat there at Lou Mitchell's after you walked out the door and I knew my whole world had just disappeared. Being with you was the only thing I dreamed of for almost five years while I was in Europe, while I was in that hospital. I couldn't just let all my hopes and dreams walk out that door."

"I'm afraid, dear Wayne, that *that* is a scene you will see over and over if you keep pursuing me," Kate said. "I am angry. You sent the book back to the home where I live with my husband and my baby. You ambushed me in front of my flat. And now you follow me halfway across this large country. What, did you quit your job?"

"No, I just took a leave of absence," he answered.

Kate was livid. "Well, go back. Go back to Chicago or go back to Manchester. Just leave me alone. You've caused me enough pain." She turned her back to him.

"Katherine, I'm so sorry I've hurt you. I just can't imagine my life without you in it. Please, darling, let me have one last word with you over dinner. I won't pressure you, I promise. I will take my leave after that. It was just too open-ended back there in Chicago. I have to say my piece before letting you go. Please, one last dinner."

Kate turned back around slowly. "We have been planning on a nice, sit-down supper in Albuquerque. All right, Wayne, but June here comes with us, so whatever you have to say will be said in front of her as well. And we'll be payin' for our own supper, thank you very much."

"I'll take that deal, my dear," he answered. "I've been reading the brochures about a nice hotel with a lovely restaurant. It's here in my motorcar. Wait here and I'll get it for you. Meet me there . . . oh, and Katherine, thank you."

He handed her the brochure and she drove off. June read the name: The Fred Harvey Alvarado Hotel. Kate glanced at the page. "That place looks far too dear for us to be stayin'," she said.

June answered, "If you mean it looks expensive, I agree. But, come on, we've been staying in motor courts every day. Just this once let's stay in a fancy place. Tell you what--I'll treat us to it. I figure by this time tomorrow we'll be in California."

"All right," Kate answered, looking bewildered.

"So tell me, what are you going to do about Wayne?" June asked.

"I'm very upset that he would follow me all this way. I thought I made myself quite clear. Jesus, Mary, and Joseph, just seeing him again made my heart do a flip, but I won't be tellin' him that."

June wrinkled her nose and pushed up her glasses. "I'm not sure what you see in him. I mean, he's handsome and all, and he talks all proper like, but he's sure not my type."

This made Kate chuckle a little. She didn't bother trying to explain how Wayne was the symbol of her youth and heritage. Part of her was afraid that he still had the power to change her mind. She was starting to regret accepting the dinner offer.

Texas

Cheryl and I saw signs for Glenrio, but as we approached, Cheryl spoke up. "Hey Kev, I thought the guy at the gas station said this was a ghost town. It doesn't look like a ghost town to me." Cheryl accessed her encyclopedia software. She rarely used it, but the Internet still had no signal. "Hey, look, we're almost in

New Mexico. Yep, says here that Glenrio is a Route 66 ghost town that was bypassed by I-40. Where the heck is I-40 anyway?"

"I don't know," I answered as I pulled onto a side road to try and find it. We crossed the railroad tracks, but after that there was nothing but plains around us in either direction. I pulled back onto the main route and headed west. When we got to the New Mexico side, the road narrowed, and it became obvious that it wasn't taken care of the way it was in Texas. But there were many more businesses here. I told Cheryl that it was probably a Route 66 preservation area.

"Maybe it's a movie set," she suggested. "Look, all the cars are pre-1950. In fact, the whole town looks like it's right out of the 1940s. Check out that ad for Lucky Strikes."

Cheryl was right. The sign had an attractive woman smoking a cigarette with the words, *"Smoke a LUCKY and feel your LEVEL best."*

"What the heck?" I said. "It must be some sort of set. They couldn't have an ad like that today. You wanna stop?"

"Nah, let's just keep going," she replied. "This place sort of gives me the creeps."

"Okay," I answered. "I imagine we'll meet up with the interstate soon, if not for anything else but our bearings. Your wireless should come back as we approach bigger towns. I thought you had that service with the big red map over your head."

I still could feel my Grandma Kate's presence along the road, but the feeling had changed somehow. I felt like she was now even closer to me. Maybe it was just because Glenrio was as it might have looked in her day.

As the storm clouds passed, the sun came out in spades and the sky turned a beautiful blue. But we started to get concerned when we noticed that all the cars on the road going in either direction were old-time vehicles. Five miles up we passed another town called Endee, and it was set up the same way, like the 1940s. Ten more miles and we were in Bard, and yes, this town looked the same as the rest.

"That's it, I'm stopping for gas." I pulled into a Texaco, and before I could get out, there were a couple of dudes surrounding the car.

115

"Filler up?" one of guys asked. I nodded. "Hey, what sort of car is this? Lookie here, Joe, you ever seen a car like this one?"

"It's a Chevy HHR," I said. "Here, I'll open the gas door." I flipped the level and the door popped open.

The attendant looked surprised. "Well, I'll be. This is one fancy automobile you got here, mister. Joe, check out that grill. That'll be a one dollar, fifty cents even."

"You filled it?" I asked.

"Yes sir, all filled up."

"And it's a buck fifty total?"

"Yes, sir. The oil's good," he added. "You want me to check the radiator?"

I pulled out two dollars, handed it to him, and told him to keep the change. "Cheryl, what just happened?"

"I don't know," she answered. "How could anyone think this is a fancy car?" Cheryl rolled down the window and yelled to the guy as he was walking away. "Excuse me, sir, could you tell me the date?"

"Sure, it's Monday the 25th," he yelled back.

"March?" she asked.

"You've been on the road so long, you don't know what month it is? Yes, ma'am, it's March 25." The two men laughed.

"Ha-ha," Cheryl laughed nervously, "you're gonna love this next question, then."

As we drove away with the answer that we were starting to fear, Cheryl exclaimed, "1946, Kevin! We're in fricken' 1946. How could this be?" We passed more store signs. Beef was 29 cents a pound. Hills Brothers coffee, 14 cents a can. Tip Top bread, 7 cents a loaf.

"I'm just glad we took my car instead of yours," I said. "I'm also glad I didn't buy one in bright yellow or something."

"That doesn't help! How could this have happened?" she snapped.

"I guess it was the storm," I answered. "Wait, don't you get it? This is how I'm supposed to save Grandma Kate. We're in her time. She's on this road somewhere. She hasn't been murdered yet."

* * * * *

As I drove on, I started to theorize, which was a dangerous thing for me. Finally, I burst out, "Cheryl, I think I got it!"

"Got what?" Cheryl was still not happy about our situation.

"The answer to time travel," I said with total confidence.

"Yeah, and what's that?"

"Water," I said.

"Water?" she asked.

"Yep," I answered. "Remember all those other experiences I had, like on the bridge? Oh, and even the old-time radio in the roadside park that *USED* to be there? Water was present in every instance."

"Have you lost it?" she quipped.

"No, listen to me, Cher. When I was on the bridge, I was concentrating on the river below. I found myself in a trancelike state, staring at the water and concentrating on Grandma Kate in 1946. I think I slipped in, but only halfway. It was similar in our storm at the park. We slipped in temporarily and saw the café and gas station that existed back in this time. Maybe the lightning somehow helped push it along. Don't you get it? This whole trip we have been concentrating on one thing and one thing alone-- finding Grandma Kate."

"Okay, so what made us slip in all the way this time?" she asked.

"I can't be a hundred percent sure," I answered. "But after finding out about the murder, both of our minds were focused on her even stronger. Then along comes the tornado with its rain and lightning. I remember staring at the water on the windshield, thinking about my grandmother, and being determined to find her." I looked over at her. "What were you thinking of at that moment?"

Her voice softened slightly as she answered, "I was thinking about Grandma Kate, too, and also her companion, June. How sad it was that two women were doing something that would have been considered very independent, especially in their day, and then were killed in the process. I was thinking how I would have liked to have been there to stop whatever happened to them."

"BINGO!" I yelled, startling her.

She looked at me. "So the secret that has been evading physicists all these years of theorizing time travel is a thing as simple as water? Give me a break."

"Well not just water, our mutual concentration too, but apparently so," I said, shrugging. "We're made of water, Cheryl. Water is life giving and for us Christians, sacramental.

It's the same water recycled since the beginning of the world. The drinking water in your bottle right there has seen all time periods. It was present in Moses's time, in Jesus's time, in Grandma Kate's time, and our own time.

"Okay, I get it, but how are we going to get back to our own time?" she asked. "Or are we?"

"I don't have the answer to that, but I guess when the time comes, we can concentrate on home and . . ."

". . . have a glass of water," she interrupted. "I guess you're right. We should concentrate on finding Grandma Kate and June, and saving them before worrying about getting home ourselves. Hey, it just occurred to me that my Bubbe Adi would be coming from Germany to Chicago about now, having been recently released from Dachau. Wow! Imagine that! Oh, and Grandpa John might be sitting in your apartment right now with your dad."

I smiled. "Wouldn't it be cool to go back to Chicago and see them all as young people?"

Cheryl crossed herself in playful mocking but in a way that let me know she actually did like the idea of seeing our relatives at about our age. They would be young and vibrant, and much different from the people we knew as children of the eighties. In any event, the one thing we did know was that we were going to meet my Grandma Kate. Of that, there could be no doubt.

"Cheryl," I continued, "I've seen enough time-travel movies to know we have to be careful not to change too much of the past. We are on a special quest to save Grandma Kate and hopefully June gets a free ride, but we can't make our presence change too much here."

"You already have," she said.

"How?"

"By giving that gas station attendant two dollars printed in the twenty-first century."

"Holy crap, you're right," I answered. "It's a good thing single dollars won't bring as much attention as the other bills with their huge dead president heads. It's a good thing I have all these singles. But how will we get a room tonight?"

We drove through Bard and received a few finger points and stares at the car, but for the most part, we went unnoticed. I was just hoping we wouldn't have a breakdown, as I didn't think I could get my onboard computer or electronic tuning repaired in 1946. Just then, my eye caught a glimpse of the unmistakable greenback color of money lying off to the side of the road. I pulled over, more out of habit, since there wasn't another car in sight. I picked it up to look, and sure enough, it was a crisp twenty-dollar bill printed in 1934. I couldn't believe it. It was like an angel or somebody put it there for us to find. Looking at it, I noticed that it didn't look much different from the bills of our time--that is, before they changed them to protect us from counterfeiters. It seemed that our quest was working out.

Chapter 10
Arizona- Don't Forget Winona

Albuquerque
March 25, 1946

Kate and June were not used to niceties like valet parking and found the Alvarado Hotel to be gorgeous. June anxiously made her way to the front desk and booked a room with two beds for her and Kate. She was thrilled but still worried about her friend and what would happen at dinner that night.

The room was elegant and worlds away from the motor courts of the past few days. It was done in Spanish motif. June pointed to the chocolates on their pillows. They even had a telephone in the room.

"Oh my, look at the view," June exclaimed, gazing out the window. "This is a wonderful city."

"Tis indeed," Kate answered. "But we best hurry to get washed up. It's getting late, and I'm rather hungry."

"I know," June answered. "Besides the peanuts, all we had was half a hamburger for lunch and that was hours ago. Oh, my God, Katherine, what am I going to wear? I didn't bring any nice dresses. I don't really own any."

"Let's see," Kate said, eyeing her friend up and down. "You're quite a bit taller than me, but your frame is about the same. I may have a nice blouse and a longer skirt. Yes, try these on."

After her shower, June came out with the borrowed clothes on. The skirt that was long on Kate looked just about right on June. It was a black skirt with silver buttons and a cream-colored blouse. Kate thought she looked nice and took it upon herself to fix up June's hair and encourage her to put on makeup. She always knew June would be pretty if she only gussied herself up a little.

Kate almost wore the same black dress she wore the night John took her out on his first night home but thought better of it. She tried on a little red number.

"Hubba-hubba," June said when she saw her. "You're the living end. But don't you think it's a bit too sexy for the occasion? Just what message would that be sending to Wayne?"

Kate looked at herself in the mirror and decided June was right. She put on a more modest forest-green dress with a white lapel and gold buttons.

June told her that it was a much better choice--although she was thinking that even in the modest dress, Kate still looked sexy. She couldn't help it; she just always did.

The man operating the elevator couldn't keep his eyes off the women as they made their way down to the lobby. "Main floor!" he called out as he stopped the lift and grabbed the lever to release the door. "Please watch your step."

As they exited the lift, there was Wayne sitting in a chair looking a bit impatient. He stood when he saw them. Kate noticed a glimmer of hope in his eyes and felt a pain in the pit of her stomach.

"Good evening, Katherine and . . . June, is it?" he asked.

"Good evening to you, Wayne," said Kate.

"Well, you're both looking lovely," Wayne stated. "Shall we? It's right this way to the dining room." He stuck out his arm to Kate, but she grabbed June's instead. June felt like a Hollywood star as Wayne pulled the chair out for her.

"Thanks, chum," she said, making him scowl at the way she spoke.

When he had seated himself, Wayne ordered a bottle of Chateau Chasse Bordeaux. "I just can't drink that American swill," he said.

"Wayne," began Kate, "so when exactly did you start wearin' a hat?"

"It's for travel, love," he answered.

June cut in. "Yeah, well shouldn't it be a cowboy hat in these parts?"

"I should leave the cowboy hats to the cowboys, dear lady," he said.

Kate chuckled to herself at the thought of Wayne in a cowboy hat. "So how's the sales business?" she asked, trying to bring Wayne back down to earth. She was thinking that he was acting a bit out of his element, much more pompous than she remembered.

"It's just temporary," he answered. "But selling brushes does make me a decent living for now. Katherine, I know I can't talk to you in the private setting in which I had hoped." He glanced at June who was already munching on a breadstick. "So I will just say what I have to say. Is this it, then? Is this how the story of Wayne and Katherine ends? We fought so many obstacles back in Dublin: my parents, your parents, our different faiths, our different backgrounds and lots in life. I just can't believe we could conquer all of that only to have it end here. I love you, Katherine. You were my first and you'll be my last."

All the while he was talking, Kate was looking away. Now she looked at him directly with her piercing blue eyes. "Wayne, we were childhood sweethearts, and yes, I love you, too. There will always be a place for you in my heart. But you have shown me total disrespect. You have not considered my feelings in any of this. You have also shown no respect for my dear husband, John, a war ally and fellow soldier, I might add. You had a hard time in the war--I understand that. It may have even affected the way you're acting now. But so did John and I love him beyond words."

Wayne sipped his wine and gathered himself before answering. "I know you are married, my darling, but I always believed it was because you thought I had died. I believed that once you realized I was alive and well, things would go back to normal. I was hoping to sweep you off your feet so you would come back to Chicago but come back with *me*. It isn't my fault that you perceived me dead."

"Wayne," she answered, "My mind is made up. I *am* going back to Chicago, but I am going back to John and Sean."

June clapped her hands, starting to feel the effects of the wine in her empty stomach.

It was getting harder and harder for Kate to keep the tears in, and one finally escaped down her cheek. But she now knew her destiny. Yes, she loved Wayne, but he was her past. John and Sean were her future, and she would go headfirst into that future.

Yes, she had made up her mind. "I'm sorry, my darling, but this is how it will have to be. I will never forget what we had, but that's it. There is another lass for you out there somewhere, I promise."

All at once Kate's appetite returned, as she felt good about herself for the first time in days. Wayne was quiet for the rest of the meal but then grew more agitated. He suddenly stood up from the table. "It isn't fair," he muttered. "It's just not right. If I can't have you, why should another man be able to?" At this, he left in a huff as the ladies continued with their meal.

When they had finished eating, June went to see the Indian museum, but Kate was anxious to go back to the room and telephone John. She let the phone ring and ring, but there was no answer. She went back downstairs to meet June in the Indian building. She would try again later.

New Mexico, U.S. 66

As we approached, Cheryl and I could see the lights of Albuquerque with large hills that seemed to frame the city. I now kept the radio on to remind myself that we were really in 1946. As we listened to Doris Day singing "Sentimental Journey," I was thinking that I was a lot more thrilled than Cheryl of the thought that we had actually time-traveled. My only concern was that we hadn't somehow missed my Grandma Kate.

It seemed strange that we had to stop to ask directions to the Alvarado Hotel instead of trusting that Cheryl could seemingly magically pull up all information at any given moment. Even here, in 1946, she had still pulled up tidbits from her encyclopedia software. I admired her so much; I just wished she could get into the thrill I was feeling at the moment.

"You know, Cheryl," I began. "Time travel has always been a fantasy of mine, to be able to see and live events from the history books."

"Oh! Like what?" she asked.

"Well, like finding out what happened to Amelia Earhart or to see exactly what took place in Dallas the day Kennedy was shot. Could I stop disasters? Could I stop Kurt Cobain from killing himself? Could I tell Captain Smith to slow down the Titanic, or put out the Chicago Fire at the O'Leary barn and even witness whether it was the cow or not?"

"You do know," she added, "that the city of Chicago has exonerated both the O'Leary family and the cow."

"Really? Well, that makes it even more of a mystery, then," I said.

"What else?" she asked.

"Could I warn John Lennon of his would-be assassin, or tell Michael Jackson, 'Dude, don't take that lethal dose tonight?' How about warning the airlines on September 11, 2001? Can I change history? Will I be able to stop Grandma Kate and June Franklin from being murdered?"

"I don't know," she answered. "I'm not sure how this all works. But I figure we can change history because we already have."

"Huh? How?" I asked.

"Think," she answered. "We bought gas that was not bought by us in 1946. There will be twenty less gallons in that pump than would have been there had we not come. Also, what about that twenty-dollar bill you found? In 1946, that money would have either been lost or found by someone else. We've changed history."

"Wow, cool!" I said, but then wondered to myself whether those changes would really change the future. Would anything we did here have an impact if and when we got back to our own time?

"So, what is our plan for saving Grandma Kate?" Cheryl asked.

"Simple," I answered. "I figure if we can catch up with them here in Albuquerque and somehow convince them not to drive through Arizona . . ."

"Yeah, that will be easy," she said with a laugh. "You'll just march up to her and say, 'Hey, I'm your future grandson and I'm here to save you.'"

"She'll think I'm a nut, won't she?" I asked.

"Good chance, dude."

"I guess I'll have to play it by ear, then. You'll help, won't you?"

"Of course, Kevin," she answered. "I might be worried about not getting back to my own time, my family, and my future plans, but right here and now, I'm here for ya."

"Future plans?" I asked.

"Never mind," she said. "I'll talk to you later. Besides, if we're stuck here, there will be a whole new set of future plans and I'll die around the time I should have been living in. But, hey, we can learn to jitterbug and see the birth of rock and roll."

I ignored her edgy sarcasm because I understood her anxiety. "So, what would you like to see if you could time-travel anywhere?"

"Well, I'd go back a lot further than you," she answered. "I would go to the Holy Land and meet Moses and Solomon and the women of the Hebrew Scriptures: Sarah, Ruth and Bathsheba. I would also like to help those in the concentration camps in Poland and Germany. I think that's what's bugging me, Kev. We're in a time that was too close to that diabolical part of history. From our vantage point here, my people were being sent to the gas chambers just last year. Part of me can enjoy the cool stuff we're seeing. On one hand, there is an innocence here that doesn't exist in our time. People go to church and temple, and have strong family values. Doris Day sings of innocence, and you won't hear the F-bomb on the radio. But then you realize that people were being treated like animals. Oh, I'm sorry, Kevin; I'll shake this. We should be getting close to the hotel. Do you think we should stop at a roadside café to eat before getting to the Alvarado?"

"Good idea," I said, still thinking about what Cheryl's concerns were. "Hey, don't worry about what you're feeling. I may be thickheaded sometimes, but I want you to know that I get it."

Sitting in the Mexican-American diner, I realized that diners like this still existed in the twenty-first century, especially in rural America. We decided on the tacos de pollo and thought the rice was cooked perfectly. I felt guilty paying the super modest price with my singles, like I was a counterfeiter or something. But I knew I had to save that twenty for the hotel.

"You know, we can't let the valet park this car," I said. "It looks old on the outside, but if he got a load of this interior and dash lights, he'd think it was something out of the comic books."

I pulled over and parked in an inconspicuous spot. As we walked toward the hotel, we started to see how beautiful it was.

"Does this place still exist in our time?" I asked Cheryl.

"Nope!" she answered. "I read it was demolished in 1970. The loss is still felt by people like us who hate to see the treasures of the past destroyed. The sad thing is, no one really knows what caused its demise. I read that it was a stop on the Santa Fe Railroad. As you are well aware, people started using air travel instead of the rails. Listen, do you hear that?"

I stopped and heard the sound of the train whistle in the distance, and this really got to me. Trains were in my blood. Here we were in a time when all of America was using the rails like in the song "On the Atchison, Topeka and the Santa Fe." In our time, just like Route 66, the rails weren't what they used to be and it changed the country somehow. Knowing me as she did, Cheryl sensed what I was feeling and put her hand in my arm as we walked. The weather was beautiful.

"I've been thinking," she started as we were almost at the front door. "We better only book one room to save money. We only have this one twenty, and it's not going to stretch very far in a place like this, even in 1946."

"Good point," I said. "We'll book as Mr. and Mrs. Bachman. Even though June booked the room, the Callahan name could cause some unknown confusion."

"Okay, Mr. Bachman," she teased. "Geez, it sounds like I'm referring to my papa."

I booked the room for two and happily got change back from my twenty.

"Excuse me, sir," I said to the clerk, "some friends of ours booked rooms here earlier. Could you tell me which room the Franklin party is occupying?"

"Certainly, it's room 115," he answered.

"Thank you," I said. "Yes, oh, and how about Peterham?"

"Let's see," he answered, looking at the guest registry. "Mr. Peterham is staying in room 17. Is there any luggage for you, Mr. Bachman?"

"No thanks, um, it will be arriving later," I answered nervously.

Cheryl and I went to the room, which was beautiful but dated. Usually, when a hotel room was dated, the fixtures and furniture looked old, but here they were dated and brand-new.

I was anxious to go meet my Grandma Kate, so we hurried to room 115. Just before I knocked, I turned to Cheryl. "Dear God, what am I going to say to her?"

"You better think of something fast, brainiac," she said. "She could walk right out that door at any moment."

I had butterflies that wouldn't quit, my saliva dried up and my tongue cleaved to the roof of my mouth.

"How's this?" she asked. "We'll just ask her to come and sit with us, tell her that we need to talk to her about an urgent matter."

"Okay, that's good; that's real good. Yes. Yes, that's what we'll say. Oh man, I'm nervous."

"Calm down," she said and knocked on the door herself. I gulped and we waited, but no one answered. She knocked again, but there was still no answer. She wasn't in the room. "Let's go walk around the hotel. She has to come back eventually."

The hotel had an old-world charm that just couldn't be found in our time. Even when hotels tried to make themselves look "vintage," it wasn't the same. Here, however, was dark sturdy furniture. The bar chairs had rounded slat backs and swiveled. The bar must have been solid walnut. We passed a complete barber shop inside the hotel, and I was thinking that I did need a haircut. Unfortunately, it was closed.

I started to relax as we walked around. I went into the small necessity shop and spotted something that I knew I had to buy for my dad. I grabbed it, pulled out the original dime I had found back in St. Louis, and paid for a brand-new 1946 Captain America comic book. He and his sidekick Bucky were fighting a Nazi character called the Red Skull. It occurred to me that this dime was with me the whole time. Did it help us make the time jump? Who knew? The one thing I did know was that if I ever got back home to my own time, a certain Mr. Sean Callahan will be very happy to see this comic.

"Planning on doing a little light reading there?" Cheryl asked, coming up behind me. But before I could answer, she said that she wanted to go to the Indian building to see the museum and gift shop.

We followed the signs, and as we anxiously turned the corner, I smacked right into a lady wearing a green dress. "Excuse me, I'm so sorry," I said to her, and as I did, I looked her right in the eyes. They were the bluest eyes I'd ever seen, and the reality of the situation became very clear. I was looking into the eyes of my

Grandma Kate. She was even more beautiful than any picture I had ever seen of her.

"And just what would you be in such a hurry about then, sir?" Her accent was like that in my dream.

"Begging your pardon, ma'am," I stammered. "We were just going to see the Indian museum."

"Well, we've just come from there," she answered, "and it doesn't close for another hour. You'll have plenty of time." She looked at me intensely, like she was trying to figure something out. "Sir, have we met before?"

"Not really," I answered nervously. "Well, in my dreams . . ."

"Oh, I've heard that one before," she quipped. "And here you are sayin' that to me and standing next to your lass." She turned to the woman standing next to her. "Men are such cads."

I was dumbfounded. "No, no, I didn't mean . . ."

Cheryl came to my rescue. "Hello, my name is Cheryl Bachman, and my friend Kevin here didn't mean what it sounded like. He has a habit of putting his feet where they don't belong, namely in his mouth. We have actually been meaning to meet and talk to you about something important. May we sit down, perhaps with a drink, and talk a bit?"

"You've been meaning to talk to me?" Kate asked.

"Yes, to both of you actually," Cheryl answered. June looked at her over her glasses.

"Well, I do need to make a telephone call," Kate said apprehensively.

"It will only take a few minutes. One drink, perhaps," Cheryl said.

Kate agreed, and we went to the bar and sat at a table. All three ladies ordered wine, but I had to try the beer. It was just Pabst but tasted nothing like the Pabst Blue Ribbon I knew. Instead, it made a nice, thick creamy head.

Cheryl started the introductions. "I'm Cheryl Bachman and this is Kevin Ca . . ." She paused.

I jumped in. "My name is Kevin Callahan, and I know that you are Mrs. Katherine Callahan. I presume that this is June Franklin." The women looked stunned and confused.

June asked, "Hey, how come you know our names? Who are you? You related to Katherine here?"

Kate cut in, "Yes, Mr. Callahan, do tell what this is all about."

"Here's the problem," I answered. "You're not going to believe our story because it's . . . well, unbelievable."

"Try me, sir. I've been around unbelievable things before." Kate's stare was unnerving.

"Just tell her, Kevin," Cheryl suggested.

"All right, here goes. I *am* related to you. You have a baby back home named Sean Callahan." Her piercing eyes made me squirm. I never realized how blue they actually were. "Well, Sean is my father, which makes me your . . ."

"Grandson!" Kate interrupted.

Cheryl continued. "We don't know how this happened, but in our time, which is nearing seventy years from now, we were on a mission to follow your path in hopes of discovering what happened to you back in 1946, and we ended up here in your time."

"*Back* in 1946?" June asked.

"Yes, this is our past," I said. "Kate, you left Chicago . . ."

"Excuse me Mr. Callahan," she said angrily, "but only me husband calls me Kate. It's Katherine or Mrs. Callahan."

"I'm sorry," I said. "Since your husband, my Grandpa John, always called you Kate, it just got passed down. You have always been Grandma Kate to me and even to Cheryl here."

"So, please continue, Mr. Callahan." Her voice was cold and businesslike.

I went on. "Well, the truth is, you left my grandfather and my father on March 22, 1946, and headed west on Route 66 to go visit my Great-Aunt Karen in California, but you never reached her house. You disappeared, and Grandpa John never fully recovered from his loss. He's in a nursing home in Chicago. We discovered that you and Mrs. Franklin may have been victims of foul play." June gasped a little.

Kate remained dead calm. "If you're from the future, Mr. Callahan, then you would know who delivered this foul play."

Cheryl answered. "Well, that's the mystery. Your car was never found, nor was any forms of identification. It was believed that maybe you left the country, so John and the police stopped the hunt. But we recently discovered that two unidentified women's bodies were found in the desert in Arizona. We are ninety nine percent sure those bodies belonged to you. We're not sure why they never put two and two together, unless Arizona just didn't . . . doesn't have good communication with the other states."

"Are you some kinda lady cop or something?" June asked.

"I am a private detective," Cheryl answered.

Kate replied, "Well, that would explain how you know so much about us and our business. Now I would like to know who put you up to this."

"Grandma Kate, I swear we are telling the truth." I crossed myself and at this

Kate scowled. "Don't be invokin' the name of the Lord in your lies, Mr. Callahan, I won't have it."

I put my face in my hands and wept a little. I kept saying, "She's got to believe me; dear God, please let her believe me." When I looked up, Kate was looking at me, a little softness now in her eyes but also confusion.

"There, there now, Mr. Callahan," she said. "If it will set your mind at ease, we will stay here and talk more in the morning. We won't go to Arizona."

"Thank God," I answered.

Kate continued, "Now, if you don't mind, I have that telephone call to make. Mr. Callahan and Miss Bachman, would you be so kind as to tell me what rooms you are staying in?"

"Yes, of course, we're both in room 55." I saw my Grandma Kate's eyebrow rise slightly.

"Thank you," she said. "Good night to you both."

Cheryl and I stayed at the bar and I ordered another beer, feeling a little relieved that even delaying her leaving could spare her life.

* * * * *

"Do you believe that cock-and-bull story, Katherine?" asked June.

"Come with me," Kate said without answering.

They walked up to the lobby's front desk.

"Excuse me, sir, I would like to see if our friends are still booked in room 55. Would you be so kind as to check for me?"

"Room 55 has Mr. and Mrs. Bachman," the clerk said.

"Yes, that's them, thank you very much. Oh, by the way, is there a way we can be awakened in the wee hours of the morning?"

"Certainly, ma'am. I can leave a message for the late night clerk to telephone your room. What time would you like to rise?"

"Four o'clock in the morning please, room 115," Kate said.

"Yes, ma'am, you will be getting a call at 4:00 a.m."

"Thank you." At this, they walked away.

"We're leaving?" asked June.

"Callahan, indeed!" quipped Kate. "Those two are married. What man would book a room in the woman's name? Don't you see? Wayne must have hired them. I am so angry, I could spit fire. I have a good mind to go knock on his door right now and give him a good piece of my mind."

"But why would they tell such a fantastic story?" June asked.

"Perhaps because they know I'm Irish and we Irish love our folktales. Come on, June."

"It's curious," June started.

"What is?" Kate asked.

"That he has the name you called out in the storm--Kevin."

Kate stopped for a moment, shook her head, and started back to their room. When they entered, June dressed for bed while Kate went back to the telephone. It rang five times before being picked up.

"Hello," came the familiar voice of her beloved husband.

"Hello, John, it's me. Oh, I've missed you so much. I want to . . ."

John's voice interrupted. "Hello, is anybody there?"

"John, my love, it's me, Kate."

"Hello, Hello? This better not be a prank--I have a sleeping baby. Hello?" The phone hung up.

Kate dialed the number again, but the operator came on and said that the number could not be reached as dialed. Kate was disheartened but warmed by the sound of her husband's voice.

Tomorrow she would be in California and would call again from Karen's home. She got dressed for bed and joined June.

"Katherine," June started, "those two scared me. I know it's a weird lie and all, but I can't help thinking about us being killed in the very place we're heading toward tomorrow."

Kate answered. "I have to admit, there was something about that man and his conviction in telling his tall tale. I was angry listening to him but got a warm feeling from him. It occurred to me when you mentioned his name that he did remind me of the fellow from my dream in the church. I got the same feeling when I was looking at him, like looking into my own baby's eyes."

"You think maybe we shouldn't go or perhaps take a different route?" June asked.

"There is no other route through the Arizona desert. Besides, I'm anxious to get to me sister's house. I miss her, and also I will finally have the time to talk to John. If you want to stay back, that's fine. I could drop you off at the train station. But I'll be leaving first thing in the mornin'."

"No, Katherine. We've come this far together, I won't abandon you now. Besides, I might meet some more great fellas." She grinned, which made Kate chuckle.

* * * * *

Cheryl and I climbed into our respective twin beds. I felt at ease knowing that I would have the chance to talk and convince my Grandma Kate to go back home to my waiting grandfather. Cheryl was unusually quiet.

"Penny for your thoughts," I said. "They're made from pure copper in this time."

"She was beautiful, wasn't she?" Cheryl asked. "Why would anyone want to harm her?"

"Dunno," I answered, fluffing the unusually soft pillow. "We still don't know if it was Wayne or not. Should we interview him?"

"I don't think so." Cheryl looked over at me. "She had . . . has everything to live for. I wonder if she knows it. She has a husband who loves her so much, he would do anything for her. She has a little baby who grows up to be a fine man and produces another fine man--you."

"Thanks, kid. Why so sad?" I asked.

"Kevin, those are the things I want for myself, for my life," she answered.

"But for the most part you do, Cheryl. You're beautiful, you have me, your best friend, who loves you, and . . ."

"And what?" she asked, louder than usual. "There is no AND--the last one is a baby. I have no baby and no way to get one in my current situation."

"You want a baby?" I asked. "Geez! Well, you could always adopt."

"Yes," she answered, "adoption is a wonderful thing, but I have what they call a biological clock ticking."

"You never really believed in that, Cher," I said.

"It's not that I didn't believe in it," she answered. "I just had never experienced it before. But I've just turned thirty-three years old, and well, that's why I have decided to marry David when . . . if I get back home."

"What? Marry David? I didn't think you loved him that much."

"I care for him a great deal, and he's a good and faithful Jewish man. He will be a good husband and father. He will give my life stability."

"Wow!" I said. "I don't know what to say. But I suppose that can be cool. We will still be friends, and the three of us can hang out at the Spaulding apartment . . . well, four of us when the baby arrives."

"No, you don't understand," she said. "David plans on moving to Israel for at least five years, and I plan on going with him."

A lump the size of a grapefruit started to form in my throat. "Cheryl, where did this come from? What about me? What about us?"

"What about *us*, Kevin?" she said, her voice suddenly turning bitter. "What about YOU? You had your chance, over and over in fact. This trip, for instance--even tonight."

"Chance for what?" I asked. "What are you talking about? What about this trip?"

"Never mind. There are things you probably will never know about me." Her voice softened. "I'm sorry. I never wanted to hurt you. You mean so much to me. Go to sleep. It may all be a moot point if I never get back to David and our own time. I promise to enjoy 1946 with you for now, since NOW seems to be all we have."

Chapter 11

New Mexico
March 26, 1946

I didn't sleep well that night thinking about Cheryl, so when sleep finally came, it came hard. When I woke, I reached for my pocket watch on the nightstand. I had to focus my eyes to see the analog dial. It was 7:45 a.m. Late for me, I thought. Cheryl was in the bathroom. As I put my watch down, the thought occurred to me that this watch was what they called a time paradox. Right now, it existed both here and also back home with Grandpa John. I was sitting up in bed, wondering how this could be, when Cheryl came back out. She was fully dressed and looked happy for a change.

"Morning," she chirped.

"Morning, how did you sleep?" I asked.

"Not bad, I think I was relieved to get that David thing off my chest with you. Come on, get dressed, and let's go find Grandma Kate. It really is extraordinary to actually be back in time. I'm taking some of these soaps. Remind me to pick up some perfume. Do you have any more of those singles left? Oh, never mind, I might have a few."

I thought as long as I lived I would never fully understand women, but I was glad to see her enjoying the time travel.

I got dressed quickly as Cheryl used the phone to dial the front desk. "May I please be connected to room 115?" she asked. Then I saw her face drop. "Are you sure? All right, thank you. This is awful."

"What is it?" I asked.

"The clerk said that the party in room 115 checked out early this morning. Kevin, they're gone."

"Damn, now what?" I asked.

"I don't know," she answered. "We've got to try and follow them."

"But, Cher, what if they went back home?"

"Then they will be safe," she answered. "But if they kept going, they could still be in grave danger."

We got our belongings together and went down to the desk to check out. As we were waiting for the clerk to finish up with another customer, we heard him address the man as Mr. Peterham. The clerk said there was a note left for him. Cheryl felt me tense and touched my arm to calm me. I felt like jumping the guy right then and there.

Cheryl knew that I would blow it, so she took charge. "Excuse me, sir, but is your name Wayne Peterham?"

"Yes, it is," he answered, "but you have me at a disadvantage, Miss . . ."

"Bachman," she stated. "May I be so bold as to ask if that note is from Katherine Callahan?"

"Yes, as a matter of fact, it is. Who are you exactly?" Wayne asked.

She put on her professional voice. "I am Detective Bachman from Chicago, and my colleague and I are investigating Mrs. Callahan's disappearance, so I will have to have a look at that note, sir."

"Of course," he answered. "I really didn't understand its content, but now I see that apparently it's about you." He handed Cheryl the note and we both read it.

Wayne,

That was a nice try, but I am not falling for the scare tactic from your hired detective team. I think it was despicable, and I never want to see your face again. I am going to see my sister Karen, and then I'm going back home to John and Sean.

Regards,
Katherine

There on the page was a postage stamp affixed sideways, toward the right.

Cheryl looked up from the page. "We know about the secret code between you and Katherine, Wayne. What does this one mean?"

"It's one I have never had from her," he answered with sadness. "It means literally, 'Do not write me anymore.' But we used to tease about that one. To receive it would be the kiss of death for us. Tell me, who did hire you? I didn't think her driving to her sister's home was a mystery to be unraveled by detectives."

Cheryl answered, "We, ah, represent John Callahan, and there is reason to believe that Mrs. Callahan is in grave danger. That's all I can say."

"Miss Bachman, if Katherine is in danger, I would like to be of assistance. I carry a pistol."

"Oh, I'm sure you do," I muttered under my breath.

"Begging your pardon, sir?" he asked, looking in my direction.

"Oh, don't mind him," Cheryl interjected. "Mr. Peterham, may I ask where you will be going from this point?"

"I was planning on heading back home. Katherine and I had words last night at dinner, and she made her intentions quite clear. I had hoped to give her this note of my own, but she had already departed."

"I don't mean to pry into your private affairs, sir, but we do need to see that note." Cheryl was still in full cop mode.

"Certainly," he said. "In fact, if you catch up with her, perhaps you can give it to her. Here it tis."

As before, we both read the note together.

Dearest Katherine,

I wanted to offer you my heartfelt apology for my behaviour. Not only in not respecting your final words in Chicago and following you across the country, but also in the bitterness I displayed last night to you and your companion. I wish for you all the best in your life.

Respectfully yours,
Wayne

There were two postage stamps affixed. One was upright, tilted to the left and positioned near the note content. The other was in the normal upright position right after his signature.

"So, explain the stamp thing then, Wayne," I said as I spoke to him for the first time.

"Certainly, sir, and you are?"

"My name is Kevin Callahan, and yes, I am a relation to John and . . ."

"To John," Cheryl interrupted quickly.

Wayne continued. "Our code is not straightforward. I will give you the literal meaning first, as passed down to me from my grandmother, and then how Katherine would have interpreted it. The stamp placed tilted to the right means 'I will be true to you.' When affixed near my written message, it means that I will be true to the promises made herein. The stamp placed upright and straight means 'ever remembered.' Placed near my signature and the words 'respectfully yours' means that I will never forget her but I will also remember to respect her wishes. We from the United Kingdom are quite a sordid bunch, aren't we?"

"Yes, quite," I said, but then I saw the painful look in his eyes. A look like I must have had the night before when Cheryl told me she was marrying David and moving away. In any event, I started to believe him and that his motives were harmless, that he would not let any harm come to Grandma Kate. I think Cheryl did too, because she gave my grandmother's note back to him.

"Thank you very much, Wayne. We will be sure to give this to Mrs. Callahan when we find her. I promise," she said.

"Thank you," he answered and walked away a defeated man. I ran after him and held out my hand, and we shook, an unspoken bond between us. He nodded, tapped his hat, and left the hotel.

"Come on, Kevin, we have to drive to Arizona and we have to drive like the wind."

Kate and June
New Mexico–Arizona

June pointed out the Rio Grande as they neared and was disappointed that it was too dark to see it. Kate was still angry at Wayne but had started to settle down for the journey by the time they reached Correo. Nothing was yet opened, and June was starting to get hungry for breakfast. As the sun began to rise behind them, they noticed how the area's inhabitants had turned from mostly western cowboy to Spanish and Indian.

At Laguna, they witnessed small Indian children setting up for selling and bartering their wares, some of them dressed in traditional garb, others in tattered rags. Off in the distance, Kate could see a white pueblo and church. She crossed herself and said a little prayer for those she loved. She now added June to her prayer list, and even though she was angry, Wayne was still addressed to the Lord as well.

When they reached Cubera, June was thrilled to see her first snow-capped mountain, for off to the right was Mount Taylor. Kate thought about stopping at the café here but noticed signs along the way for good food and accommodations about five miles up the road at San Fidel. It was there she stopped at a nice little roadside café. As the waitress motioned them toward a table, they found the smells intoxicating. They both ordered coffee and the special, which was hotcakes, eggs, sausage links, and potatoes.

"Katherine, it's good to be back on the road, but I keep thinking about what those two people said and it frightens me a little."

Kate was thinking about them also but didn't want to add to June's apprehension. "We'll be fine. Don't be forgettin' that we have our guardian angels with us. Besides, who would want to hurt us? Surely not these nice native people."

"I suppose you're right . . . wow these hotcakes are delicious!" June said.

Kate went back to thinking about the man named Kevin. There was something in his eyes, something about his face from her dream. He was either the greatest actor she had ever met or he genuinely cared. He had the same look of concern that she had seen so many times from John when he was worried about her.

As June stood in line to pay behind some truck drivers, Kate walked outside into the crisp New Mexico morning air. She looked down to see a small Indian boy selling little clay pots. Stooping down, she asked him how much they were. He handed one to her and she saw the price of twenty-five cents on the bottom. She placed a dollar in his hand and grabbed one for June. They were white and brown Acoma style, perfectly crafted and painted. She thought of her own son, Sean, as the boy looked up and smiled at her. He never spoke a word.

With a nice breakfast in them, the two women settled in for the beautiful drive across New Mexico. June switched on the radio and found a station playing a mixture of western and popular band music. "Katherine, the radio only gives us world and local news, but one of those truck drivers told me that in order to get news from Chicago or anywhere else, we should go to one of the many trading posts along the way."

"What exactly is a trading post?" asked Kate.

"I'm not really sure," June answered. "The driver indicated that they were started years ago by the early settlers of the West. You can buy and trade stuff there, but before the days of radio and daily newspapers, that's where people out here got their news. He said they still do the same thing. Just look at all the signs for them here."

"That's interesting," said Kate, "but what is it that you'd be wantin' to know?"

"Well, I started by asking that truck driver if he knew of Jim Schuster."

"Oh, you mean your root beer fellow?"

"Well, I was just curious," June replied. "I also asked about Rocky, but he never did say his last name, did he?"

"Not that I recall, but I think it's best you don't think about that one."

"Anyway," June went on, ignoring Kate's comment, "the driver didn't know either of them, and that's when he gave me the trading post idea. They are also supposed to have nice things to buy."

"Now, listen," Kate answered, "there will be plenty of things to buy in California. My sister Karen loves to shop. We will walk down Hollywood Boulevard and maybe see a movie star or two. Won't that be grand?"

"I guess so," June answered but turned her head with a pout. She turned the radio up and they spoke little all the way to Gallup.

Kevin and Cheryl

"You know, Cheryl, I don't even know what Grandma Kate's car looks like. I never saw a picture of it. I just know that it's a 36 Buick. I come from a long line of GM car drivers, but all the cars here sort of look-alike to me."

Cheryl was busy looking out the window and searching her encyclopedia. "Didn't you see it on the bridge when you had your vision?"

"It was dark, and I only saw the tiny taillights," I answered. "How are we ever going to find her?"

"We have to have faith, Kevin. We know where she's heading and we know where they ended up, but remember, that could have all been changed with our intervention."

"How exactly?" I asked.

"Elementary, my dear Callahan," she mocked. "We got her angry at Wayne, which caused them to leave early, mainly to avoid having to talk to us and to him."

"Yes," I answered. "But we don't know if she would have left early anyway, just to avoid him. Or how do we know that we didn't cause it in the first place."

Cheryl scrunched up her nose. "You have a point there. I guess we don't know for sure, but we'll find her. It's our mission."

"Yeah, let's just hope we find her alive," I said.

We wanted to save time and not stop for breakfast, so we ate protein bars and other snacks we had in the car. Cheryl got tired of listening to 1940s music, so I put in an MP3 playlist I had made just prior to the trip. It ranged from my parents' stuff like Pink Floyd to the Decemberists and everything in between. I played it on random. I was pushing ninety miles per hour and wondered how the traffic cops were in this part, in this time period.

Just after Santa Maria, we hit what the sign called a lava flow: black, hardened lava on both sides of the road. I found the structures they created very impressive and wondered how long ago they were formed. Before I could ask the question, Cheryl had it from her encyclopedia. "The Malpais, which is what it is sometimes called, was formed about eight hundred years ago and extends for about sixty miles to the south. 'Malpais' is Spanish for 'Badlands.'"

"Very impressive," I muttered.

"What, the lava or my encyclopedia skills?" she asked.

"Both."

At this, she huffed on her nails and polished them on her blouse. My thoughts turned to her. Her cuteness had made me laugh many times over the years. I pretended to look out the passenger-side window, but I was looking at her face and shiny blond hair. She was pretty. I guess I always just took that for granted. I never felt jealous, because she was always there. Like she belonged to me somehow, yet we never had a commitment. I was wrong for assuming it would always be like that. It was like the old saying: I thought I could have my cake and eat it, too. I never understood where a saying like that came from until now.

I gazed down at her feminine hands. Her skin was soft. Those were the same hands that had comforted me when I was sad, the same hands that had poked me playfully and knocked on my door almost daily. Now it was as if they belong to someone else. David would hold them and be comforted by them, because he would place a ring on her finger and take her far away from me and the only life I had know all these years. The sadness I felt was overwhelming, but then my Grandma Kate came to mind and I had to snap out of my self-pity.

It wasn't long before we saw a sign that read the Great Continental Divide. I had started watching the trains and the hundreds of miles of tracks that the great railroad men of the past laid down for us. It also occurred to me that my electronic skills would be null and void in this time period. I would have to work the rail like my dad and Grandpa John did, although Grandpa John didn't often leave the Chicago area. Sadly, my grandfather never became an engineer as was his dream. Chicago was the center of the railroads, then more than now. I meant now more than . . . oh, this time-travel thing was confusing.

All I knew was that it now felt good being in the Southwest in a simpler time and sharing it with Cheryl. The weather and the scenery were gorgeous. The sun filtering through the car windshield made me feel like a kid on a summer trip with my parents. Maybe we even took Route 66 back then, although it was probably the interstate. I actually wanted to turn off the radio and just soak it all in, but Cheryl seemed to be enjoying the music as she sang along to an Amy Winehouse tune. I patted her leg and went back to driving. She smiled at me briefly and then turned to look out the window.

Kate and June
Gallup

Kate pulled into a filling station just before the Gallup city limits. June returned to the car after using the lavatory. Kate came back moments later with some Hostess cupcakes and two bottles of Coca-Cola.

"The man in there said that if we are lucky, we might catch a glimpse of Spencer Tracy and Katherine Hepburn," Kate said.

"What, really?" June asked.

"Indeed, he said they are filming a picture near here."

June's eyes widened. "Neat! What's it about?"

"He didn't know for certain," answered Kate. "Sort of like a western serial. Should be showing next year. We'll have to go see it."

June smiled at Kate. "That will be swell, but this time it will be your turn to buy the popcorn."

Kate's tone changed. "Listen, June, if you really want to stop in at one of those trading post places, we will, but I just want to get some miles between us and Wayne in the event that he plans on following us again. I feel like this trip is taking forever, and I've just been anxious to get to my sister. I keep thinking that we'll be makin' the long drive home as well. Will I be taking you back to Decatur, or will you come and stay with John and me for a time?"

"Oh, I haven't thought that far ahead," June answered. "I do miss my parents, but really, I'm not in any hurry to get back home, except to see if there's a letter from Jim waiting for me. I'm still thinking about my move to Oklahoma. I guess I'll have to start making arrangements."

Gallup was a true western town with grand old buildings. Kate and June could almost imagine a gunfight breaking out in the middle of town and swinging doors on the saloon. But along with this image were shiny new 1946 cars and storefronts. June thought it was marvelous but was disappointed that she didn't get to see the movie being filmed. She swore she saw Spencer Tracy walking outside of a beautiful hotel called the El Rancho, but she couldn't be sure. Looking at her map, she realized they would be in Arizona soon.

"Katherine, we will stop to see the Grand Canyon, won't we?" June asked.

"Yes, sweetie, I suppose that is something we just can't miss now, can we?" Kate answered.

June gave Kate's shoulder a gentle rub. "I still feel bad that we used to have words back at Bruning. We fought over a comment I made about you losing your baby. When I think back, it was such a horrid thing to say. Please know how sorry I am for that."

"I'm startin' to get over that," Kate said. "I know you've had a hard time of it. For a moment, when I saw you at the hospital door, part of the hurt disappeared. You were there for me, and I'll never forget it."

"Thank you for saying that," June continued. "I wanted you to know that when we had that fight, I had just found out that I couldn't have children of my own. Frank and I tried for two years before he was shipped out. I went to the doctor and he told me I was barren. I hated you when you were pregnant that first time."

"I understand, really. You need not delve into it," Kate answered.

"No, Katherine, let me talk. There's something I need to tell you. I hated you, but I was also fascinated by you. Like I told you before, you had everything in my mind. You had unbelievable beauty, a great husband, the people at Bruning loved you, and then you were going to have a baby. I found myself having an attraction to you that I didn't understand. You know, like the women we used to see on Belmont Avenue."

"I don't understand--you were attracted to me like to a man?" Kate asked.

June's voice sounded shaky. "I thought so, but I didn't really understand it. That's why I came to help you. I used to think about you. I was so lonely after Frank died. I know you are a woman of faith, so I hope you don't think too badly of me, but I even took up with another girl for a time."

"I had no idea," Kate answered calmly, "but I'm not the sort to be judging. Your business is just that. I do not think badly of you at all."

June continued, "I thought it was what I wanted, but it really wasn't. She was pretty and she was gentle, and I was just so lonely and men didn't seem to care about me. But since I've been here on the road with you, I've discovered something about myself: I like men. What I felt for you was because you were everything I wished I was. So it wasn't that I wanted you like I would a man; it's that I really wanted to *be* you. I still do a little. But those truck drivers made me realize that I can still be a desirable woman and attract men like a magnet."

Kate laughed, "Indeed, you can. And when you're out on your own, whether it's in Chicago or Oklahoma, you'll have to beat them off with a stick."

"Why would I want to beat them away?" said June, and they both laughed. Kate squeezed June's hand slightly before placing hers back on the steering wheel.

"June, the people of Bruning, including myself, need to apologize to you. We just saw you as a bitter woman who liked to keep to herself. One just doesn't realize what's going on inside a person. So I am officially apologizing for not trying to understand you or getting' to know you better back then. But now I know you, and I see that you are a kind, caring person. I think you are as pretty as a flower, and that's what those drivers saw, too. Just be careful around certain men."

"I will, and thanks." June was silent for a moment but then added, "I'm glad you were able to have your Sean. I can't wait to meet him."

"Oh yes," said Kate. "I really want you to. There is something about a baby's love that is so pure and unconditional. I imagine that's how God's love is. I miss my wee baby, June, and my husband as well. Sometimes I think that leaving for this trip was the stupidest thing I've ever done, but then I wouldn't have gotten to know you like this. I suppose there's a purpose for everything."

"Yeah, and you wouldn't have gotten to figure out your feelings for Wayne," June said. "Sheesh, what an ass."

"No," snapped Kate. "You mustn't say such things. I know I am angry, but Wayne went through a lot in the war. We women back home sometimes don't realize what the soldiers overseas have gone through. He was almost killed. I was the anchor that he used to fight his way back from the grips of death in that hospital room. A person can become obsessed when that happens. Not that it totally justifies what he did, but I think Wayne is a good man and I will be prayin' for him."

"Well, I hope you're right," June answered. "You might change your mind if we find out he's still on our trail."

Once they drove over the state line arch into Arizona, the terrain changed. They started to see evidence of what was called the Painted Desert, with its breathtaking colors. June pulled out the soft drinks they had purchased at the filling station and, upon opening them, handed one to Kate. Even with all four windows rolled down, the heat was starting to fry them. But as they drove on, they saw that life was good in this particular moment. They had Coca-Cola, unbelievable beauty surrounding them, and each other's newfound friendship to bring them comfort.

Chapter 11
Kingman...

Arizona
Kevin and Cheryl

The state line arch was amazing, and I was sure it didn't exist in our time. This was the way a state line crossing should be. The arch was visible for a couple of miles, with its giant Route 66 shield on top. It was fantastic!

Cheryl suggested that we stop for something to drink, since we had downed the last water bottle and the heat was becoming evident.

I waited to stop until we reached Houck about twenty miles in. We didn't need gas yet, so I parked a little out of the way so to not bring attention to my HHR from the Navajo men who stood around the trading post. At least I thought they were Navajo from the posted signs advertising their silver work. They looked serious and it scared me, but as we got closer, we found them welcoming. We entered the trading post and looked around. There were all sorts of things for trade or sale. We saw men sitting in a corner, playing checkers and drinking pop, and a woman in another corner selling beautiful silver jewelry. She had a belt buckle I would have really liked to buy, but knew I had to save my passable currency. It was silver with turquoise inlay, and it appealed to me. It wasn't as gaudy as modern ones tended to be.

"Trade?" she said to me as I started to walk away.

"Trade?" I repeated.

"Yes, have you anything to trade for the buckle?" she asked.

"Let me think about that." I found Cheryl. "Do I have anything I can trade this woman for a silver belt buckle."

"Why?" she asked.

"I don't know," I answered, a little embarrassed. "I just think it would be fun. I like it."

Cheryl went out to the car and brought in a bottle of perfume, barely used. It was CK Be, and she handed it to the women who sprayed it on her arm and smiled. Cheryl asked if we could have the belt buckle and two bottles of Coke for the perfume. The deal was made, and not only did we get what Cheryl had asked for, but a leather belt was part of the deal.

I thought that was a really kind thing Cheryl had done for me, and I thanked her as I put my new belt on. Who else would spoil me by giving into my childish notions? I used a dollar to buy two more bottles of Coke, and we took off.

Holbrook was a town that was built to directly cater to passengers of the Atlantic–Pacific railroad and had thrived because of Route 66. It was strange to think that the famous Wigwam Motel wouldn't be built here for another four years. The Mother Road was built in stages, layers of history for which we were only catching a pinpointed moment. The trading posts and other businesses that stretched along the road through the beautiful Painted Desert would lie as a graveled ghost road in our time. But here in 1946, it was alive and well used. Even though the construction of the modern interstate would have already been started in places like Missouri, it was decades away here in Arizona. The thought made me sad. I wish I could somehow stop it, tell the road commissioners that so much of what made America great will be lost with its technology, that it will just add to the whole frenzy of "rush, rush, rush." The interstate did to Route 66 what air travel did to the railroad. "Hurry up and get there, and hurry back home." What resulted was that the wonderful country in between got lost in the shuffle. So even if Cheryl and I got stuck in this time, it would be extra sad just knowing what's coming, what lies ahead.

One thing I did know: if water made time travel possible, then we wouldn't be getting home via Arizona. It was dry and hot with not a cloud in the sky.

Ever since I had filled the car with gas, I could feel the difference. It was probably leaded gas, and I thought I should have asked for Ethyl. I stepped on the pedal and got the car up to a hundred miles per hour on the wide open road. We had wasted a little time at the trading post and I had to catch up with Grandma Kate.

I was thinking about how kind Cheryl was to trade her perfume for me, but when the thought about her and David came to my mind, I shoved it out of my head again. It was much too painful to dwell on. But here we were in 1946 together, and I hung onto this moment. There would be time to sort out my thoughts later.

I looked over at Cheryl who was deep in thought as well. "Dollar for your thoughts, kiddo?" I asked. "Inflation, you know."

"Oh, it's just that I saw a sign that saddened me," she answered. "It read War Relocation Camp."

"War Relocation Camp? What's that?" I asked.

"In 1942, President Roosevelt signed an executive order that moved nearly 120,000 Japanese and Japanese Americans into ten isolated relocation centers. Arizona was one of the states that had these camps. In 1946, they would have still been living in them here in the West. It won't be until 1948 that they will sign a bill to compensate these people for the loss of their property. So they are living in small huts, getting increasingly depressed. It was a sad thing, Kev. I saw pictures once of happy Americans holding newspaper headlines that read 'JAPS OUSTED.'"

"Yeah," I said, "but Pearl Harbor hit a lot of people hard. We were attacked on American soil and nobody saw it coming. It wasn't much different than our own September 11."

"Yes, but we didn't put Islamic Americans in camps," she noted.

"That's because we learned from the past," I answered.

She looked at me. "But you know there were still people who would have liked to do that."

"That's because they were hurt, just like the people here in this time. They just didn't know how to handle the war. They had no idea if there were spies all over America. Didn't someone apologize to the Japanese people years later?"

"That was Ronald Reagan in 1988. It took them long enough," she said.

We traveled through miles of winding road and the terrain kept changing. It went from desert to pine forest and back again. We passed through the Mormon town of Joseph City, which was massive farmland, and finally came to Winslow.

Cheryl asked me what song had Winslow, Arizona, in it. When I told her it was the Eagles/Jackson Brown song "Take it Easy," she started singing, *"Standing on the corner in Winslow, Arizona . . ."*

149

I interrupted her. "Did you know that Winslow was another great railroad town? It was even named after the president of the railroad at the time, General Edward F. Winslow."

"That's very interesting, Kevin," she said.

"Cheryl, why?" I blurted out.

"Why, what?" she asked.

"Why do you have to leave? I mean, I guess I can understand you wanting to get married and have babies and all, but why do you have to go to Israel?"

"Providing we get back to our own time," she started, "all Jews who are lucky enough and can afford it, long to go and study in the Holy Land--you know that. Besides, it is where my future husband has planned to go for years. With our combined income, we will now have the means."

"But five years is so long," I said, sounding defeated.

She continued, "It could be four or it could be ten. The truth is, we may never come back, or we might find it isn't for us and be back in six months. The possibilities are open to us, but I would love to broaden my studies of ancient Hebrew at the source."

"But Cher, I will . . . I can't . . . I . . ."

"What? Say it," she prodded.

I slammed shut the iron gate once again. "Never mind, Cheryl."

"Oy, you infuriate me," she quipped.

"Why, what did I do?"

"Never mind, Kevin," she said, mocking me, and turned to look out the window.

I felt I would never understand women. But I was also having trouble with my own feelings about this situation with her. It was more than just knowing she was throwing a twenty-five-plus-year friendship out the window. Why couldn't she see how much I would miss her? What did she want of me?

Cheryl decided to switch off the MP3 after a Death Cab for Cutie song ended and turned on the radio. There was a scat song by Ella Fitzgerald called "Flying Home" that caught our attention. Lady Ella had a voice that could melt carbon steel. At that moment, I wished it was Christmas time so I could hear her sing, "What Are You Doing New Year's Eve." I mentioned this to

Cheryl, but she reminded me that she wouldn't be recording that until sometime in the 1960s. I was happy to hear Ella because her voice seemed to calm our spirits as we drove through the red rock portion of Arizona.

It seemed strange to pass right by the Grand Canyon and not stop to see it, and I wondered if there would be any noticeable difference in 1946 compared to our own time. It took millions of years for the Colorado River to gouge it out, so I highly doubted it. I was sure that Niagara Falls would look different, but not the Grand Canyon. Cheryl agreed that we needed to forge ahead to try and catch up with Grandma Kate. It was worrying both of us and was a source of great tension.

"Hey, what ever happened to your sixth sense when it came to tracking your grandmother?" she asked.

I was wondering that myself. I could still feel her presence, but being in the same time with her had changed it considerably. "I guess we'll have to rely on good old-fashioned gumshoe tactics."

"Gumshoe, Kevin?" she asked.

"Yeah, well, I guess I'm acclimating to the time line," I said. "In any event, we'll have to rely on your special talents for the job. So what do we do at this point, besides just driving toward Kingman? Ask at every gas station?"

"I've been thinking about that," she answered. "Gas stations are okay, but more likely, we should be stopping at the trading posts. They were a source of passing information even before the telegraph, sort of a gossip network."

"Shouldn't we have asked back there in Houck, then?" I asked.

"Um, I did," she answered with a smirk, "while you were looking at belt buckles. They hadn't heard of two women traveling alone but suggested we go to the one near Williams."

"I should have known. Okay, on to Williams, then."

In our time, they had a steam engine with Pullman cars that took visitors from Williams to the Grand Canyon. But here in 1946, they were still using a few steam engines for real instead of just for tours, although diesel was taking over rapidly.

"Kevin, can you pull over for a minute so I can borrow your denim shirt?" she asked. "Do you mind?"

"It's fine, but why?" I said.

"People look at me strangely with this blouse on, and since I don't have any period dress, I will look more natural in jeans and your shirt, at least out here in the West."

She went into my suitcase and then changed in the backseat. I tried not to look but found myself peeking though the rearview mirror. She caught me but didn't say anything. When she got out, she tied the shirt tails in front, and sure enough, she looked like a true western cowgirl.

"Now all you need is a cowboy hat," I said.

"I think I'll pass on that," she answered. "Thanks for the shirt."

Back in 1946, Williams was already big in tourism and catered to the Grand Canyon crowd. It made me happy that it was one of the Route 66 towns that remained after the interstate bypassed it. In fact, in our time, Arizona had the longest, well-used portion of Historic Route 66 than any other state. But it was great to be here on the road before its decommissioning. There were still some old brown route shields here. I would have loved to take one home with me.

We stopped at the Grand Canyon trading post just outside of Williams. An old man in a cowboy hat talked to us. I just knew that this old cowboy was probably here during the real Wild West days.

"Howdy folks, what kin I do ya for?" he asked.

"Ah, howdy," I answered. "I was wondering if two women traveling alone came in here. We really need to find them."

"Nope, haven't seen them, but word has it they were asking some questions at Ash Fork," he answered.

"Ash Fork?" I asked.

"Yup. Trading community about seventeen miles west of here. They say one had an Irish accent."

"Yes, that's them all right," I said.

Cheryl stepped in. "Is there anything else? Do you know what questions they were asking? Do you know where they would be right now?"

"Nope," he answered, "ceptin' they were headin' for California. They might know more in Ash Fork, young lady."

As we left, there was a teenage boy peering in the window of our car. "Holy mackerel, mister, what kind of automobile is this?" he asked. "And what in tarnation is that thing?" He was looking at Cheryl's laptop left partially opened on the front seat.

"This car is a Chevrolet and that is a sort of portable typewriter," I answered.

"Geez," the boy answered, "I never saw a typewriter like that before. Where do you put the paper? Where is the ribbon?"

"Oh, it's a new kind," Cheryl explained. "Stick around, kid. You won't see this stuff for a while--top secret, you know. But you'll know what it is one day." She scuffed up the hair on the top of his head. "I saw that in a movie once," she whispered to me.

We got back in the car with the wide-eyed kid still trying to look inside. He started to ask something, but we closed the doors and drove off. Next stop, Ash Fork.

Kate and June
Arizona

It was a clear day, free of haze, as the ladies looked over the south rim of the Grand Canyon. Kate gasped, "June, have you ever seen anything with such grandeur?"

"It doesn't look real, does it?" June started. "Like, I don't know. It's not like the photos or picture shows. I think it's the most breathtaking sight I've ever seen."

"I know," Kate answered. "It's like my mind can't take it all in. Oh, I wish John were here to see this with us. He's always wanted to be here."

"Well, you'll have to have him bring you back here," suggested June.

"I could stay here all day in this one spot and look at the wonder of God's creation," Kate said.

"I know what you're going to say, Katherine. We need to get going. Thank you for stopping and staying as long as we did."

"You're quite welcome," Kate answered, finding it hard to pry her eyes away from the Canyon. "Besides, I still promised you a stop at one of those tradin' posts."

June's eyes widened into a smile that shone right through her horn-rimmed glasses.

They got back on the old faithful Highway 66, and once past Williams, Kate and June started to get thirsty again. Kate wished she had thought to bring a canteen. She thought to herself that the sodas June was so fond of were all right in a pinch, but the sugar had a tendency to make her even more parched.

At Ash Fork, they pulled into the largest trading post, and June was eager to look around. Kate found the canteen she had just wished for. June spotted a group of truck drivers who seemed to be regulars. She walked up to them. "Excuse me, fellas," she said in a meek little voice. She noticed they were big and burly. The men looked up from their coffee, cigarettes, and cards.

"Howdy, pretty lady, what can I do fer ya?" one of the men asked.

June blushed. "I was wondering if you knew a driver by the name of Jim Schuster."

"Yes, ma'am, I know Jim," the man answered. "Was in here just a day or two ago."

June's face lit up. "Really, do you know where he might be now?"

One of the other guys interrupted, "He was headin' west. Not sure exactly where. He's back and forth on this road all the time. He's an interstate driver, unlike us who pretty much stay put in Arizona."

"Thank you very much," June said, but then added, "Oh, would you happen to know a man by the name of Rocky? I don't know his last name."

The men laughed. "Nobody knows Rocky's last name--not sure he has one. Yup, we know Rocky, too. Likes to hang out at a bar called the Bon Ton Saloon in Kingman. Nice guy, lessin' he's drinkin'. Then he likes to start fights."

One of the other men jumped in. "How 'bout you, doll face? You free tonight?"

"Mind yer manners," the first driver said. "Can't you see this here is a lady?"

June answered with a smile. "Aw, you can't blame a fella for trying, but sorry, me and my friend here are heading for California."

"Well, the name's Pete, Pete Silvers, if you change yer mind. Maybe I'll see ya at the Bon Ton if'n ya stop in looking for yer friends."

"Yeah," said a third guy, "and you can introduce me to the skirt with the dark hair."

June found a pair of earrings that caught her fancy. As she paid for them, she got the address of the Bon Ton Saloon. She hatched a scheming idea and launched it once they were back in the car.

Kate asked, "So what were you talkin' to those men about?"

"Oh, just chitchat," June answered. "I got asked out again, but don't worry, I politely turned them down."

"Well, that's good, June. You can't be too careful around men, especially when they are a bit . . . hungry, if you be catchin' my meaning."

"Oh, they were nice enough," June answered. "By the way, they told me about a nice place to eat in Kingman."

"A café?" Kate asked.

"Well, sort of," June fibbed. "It's called the Bon Ton. It's right on the highway at Beale Street."

"All right dear, we do need to stop and eat. We can't live on just peanuts and cupcakes," Kate said.

June smiled to herself all the way to Kingman.

"Did you know that the cowboy actor Andy Devine was raised here?" June asked as they pulled into town. "Oh, look, there's the Bon Ton. Let's go."

Kate pulled over and read the sign. "June, this is a saloon. Do you think it's wise?"

But June had already exited the car. "Come on, I'm starved."

Kate followed June in and saw that there were other women in the saloon. The place looked like it was right from the Wild West days. At first, all eyes were on them, but as they took a seat at a nearby table, folks went back to their business. June was busy looking around.

When Kate spotted a group of truck drivers, she turned to June. "Do you really think I was born yesterday, sweetheart?"

"What on earth do you mean, Katherine?" June grinned at Kate with extra teeth showing.

"June!" Kate was looking at her with steel, blue eyes.

"Oh, all right," June answered. She hated when Kate looked at her that way. "I heard that Rocky comes here, and I figured there is a chance that Jim might frequent the joint, too. It seems to be a favorite among cross-country drivers. We had to stop to eat anyway. Please don't be sore with me, Katherine."

Kate sighed and then smiled at June to let her know that it was okay. But she was still a little nervous. It was then that she saw that the ladies in the saloon were all of a certain type, what John would call working girls.

"What's good?" June asked the bartender who was also serving as waiter.

"Ma'am, we serve up the finest chuck wagon-style steak in the West. You can also get a hamburger."

"Do you have fish?" asked Kate.

The man looked at her like she had two heads. "No, ma'am, this here is cattle country. You can get baked or French-fried potatoes."

They both ordered steak, and the man sent a barmaid off to the cellar to find a bottle of wine, which she opened and poured for the ladies. She explained to them that they mostly served whiskey and beer, and that it had been a long time since anyone had ordered wine. The bottle had no label, but Kate thought it was pretty good.

The men in the corner were still watching them. After the ladies had finished their meal, they sat back to drink their wine. Out of the darkened corner walked a man they immediately recognized. He staggered slightly toward them. "Rocky!" June exclaimed.

"Howdy ma'am, but you have me at a disadvantage," Rocky looked from Kate to June. "Hold on a minute, I recognize you, doll. You and your Scottish friend here were back there in Marshfield." Kate rolled her eyes. "You ready to cut that rug now?" he asked, still looking at June.

"We are still on our way to California," June answered. "No time for dancing, but it's nice to see you."

"Likewise," he answered.

She followed up. "Who knows, maybe we'll catch up again sometime. Hey, I was wondering if you knew a driver by the name of Jim Schuster."

"Jimmy, yeah I know Jimmy," he answered. "Whatda ya want with a bum like that? You wouldn't pick Jimmy over me, now would you? I assure you, sweet tomato, that I'm a much better dancer."

"I'm sure you are, Rocky," said June with a wink, "but I was just wondering if you knew his whereabouts just the same."

Kate was impressed by the way June handled herself with these drivers. She seemed to understand them. It was no wonder they were instinctively drawn to her.

"Yeah, doll, I see him all the time. He even comes in here once in a while. Look, I'm not just yankin' yer chain. It's best you don't hang out with ole Jimmy."

"Oh, and why is that?" June asked.

"Cause . . ." Rocky started to answer, but a couple of other men came barging up to the table. They were drunk and smelled bad. Rocky didn't seem to know them as they pushed him aside.

"Lookie here, Joe," one of the men started, "we don't get such high-falutent, split tails here in the Bon Ton. Nice to have some fresh meat around here."

Rocky tried to push himself between the men and the ladies, but the one called Joe socked him, causing him to fly and crash into the table next to them.

One of the working girls hurried to the table. "Come on, fellas, these here are nice girls. You mosey on away now. Tell you what, I'll buy you a drink and go upstairs with ya myself."

"You didn't hear me," the first man said. "I have an appetite for some new meat. These nice girls, as you put it, wouldn't be in here ifin they didn't want the same thing. Come on, Joe, we'll take them to the usual place."

At that, the men grabbed the women who started screaming and fighting back. Rocky tried to go after them, but they were joined by a third man who punched Rocky square in the face, knocking him out cold. The men shoved the women in the back of an old Ford and pulled a knife on them. Before driving off, one of them threw Kate's handbag to the third guy and told him to follow along in the women's car. The two cars drove off.

Kevin and Cheryl

Parallel Roads (Lost on Route 66)

After leaving the trading post at Ash Fork with the info and the names of the drivers June had asked about, Cheryl and I sped away toward Kingman. But instead of stopping at the Bon Ton as planned, I got the strongest feeling of doom as we neared the crossroad at Old Trails Road. I turned south on the trail.

"What are you doing?" Cheryl asked with trepidation. "Where are you going?"

But I couldn't explain it. I felt my grandmother's presence like I used to, but it was different this time. It was as if she were screaming out to me. I felt we were going to find her down this road. I just hoped it wasn't too late.

Cheryl didn't know that I made a secret purchase at the Ash Fork trading post as she was questioning the drivers. I had traded my old Timex wristwatch for a .38 special handgun. I knew that Cheryl would not approve and would probably freak out if she even suspected, even though as an officer of the law, she used to be required to carry one and test every year on its use. She still owned the gun, but as a private detective, she no longer carried it. I had loaded the gun and hidden it in my pants, wearing my shirt untucked over it. I wasn't that big into guns, but I had been thinking about it ever since Wayne told us he was carrying one.

"Well," Cheryl answered as I silently persevered on my course, "I've trusted your instincts to get us this far. I just hope you're right and they're not back there at that saloon."

The hot sun was starting to set as we drove down the old dirt trail. I was feeling nervous and worried. Had I made the right choice? But her screaming presence was still all around me.

* * * * *

The men were so drunk they swerved all over the dirt road until they pulled behind an old deserted brick building. The man driving Kate's car grabbed her out of the Ford and forced her into her own Buick, leaving the one called Joe with June. They yelled to the third man to keep watch.

"Please don't hurt me," pleaded June. "I'm a widow."

"Well, then, call me the widow *maker*." Joe laughed at his own nonsensical joke. "Come on, widow, I like it when they fight back." He started ripping off June's blouse, and his knife cut her shoulder in the process. She screamed, which just excited Joe even more. Just then the man keeping watch yelled, "Hey, there's someone coming." The men held their hands tightly over the women's mouths. They watched closely as the car stopped and saw a shadow get out and approach the Ford.

The door of the Ford swung open and the figure yelled at Joe. "Get out, what the hell do you think you're doing?" He dragged Joe out of the car and got in himself, locking the doors. "Are you all right, ma'am?" June looked at him and realized it was Jim Schuster, her Jim. She was so relieved.

"Jim, it's me June, remember?"

Jim looked at her for a moment before recognizing her. "Oh yeah, I remember."

June buried herself in his arms. He smelled like whisky and sweat, but she didn't care. She was safe. He rubbed her hair to comfort her and then started to caress her exposed skin and breasts.

"Jim, what are you doing?" she asked.

"Come on now, June," Jim slurred. "Don't you think you owe me a little something for saving you?"

"Jim, you're drunk. Please, you have to save my friend Katherine in the other car."

"Oh, your friend can take care of herself. Come on, it's been lonely driving that truck." He started kissing her sloppily all over and clutching at her breasts.

"Jim, PLEASE," she yelled and started to fight him. Just then he backhanded her across the face.

"Now you listen to me," he yelled. "We're going to have a little fun and you best not fight it."

June struggled and screamed as he ripped at her clothes, beating her over and over until she quit moving all together. He shook her limp body several times before getting out of the car.

"What the hell, Jim," said Joe." I was here first. Shit! Now look at her, she dead or something? SHIT!"

Jim staggered over to Kate's car where he saw the man slowly taunting her with his knife. He had enjoyed slowly cutting off her blouse buttons one by one and had just cut off her brassiere. Her wrists were tied behind her back. Kate had her head down and refused to look at the man or show any signs of fear, which was infuriating him. Jim yanked open the car door and pulled Kate out.

"What the fuck do you think you're doing, Jim?" the man yelled.

"Get rid of this car, I think the other dame is dead," Jim said callously.

"What? What the fuck is wrong with you, Jim?"

"Just get rid of this car so nobody can ever find it," yelled Jim. "We'll have to take care of this one, too. She's seen our faces."

Kate uttered no sound but looked up dead cold into Jim's face. If she could have killed him right then and there, she would have.

He continued, "But first I'm gonna have a little fun with her. Hopefully, she won't die on me first." He grabbed at her exposed breasts. "Quit looking at me," he yelled at Kate, "or I'll have to get me a blindfold."

Just as Kate's car was driven off, Joe and the lookout man came walking up holding onto two people.

"Lookie what we found trying to sneak up," said Joe. "This one had a gun."

I saw Grandma Kate look up at us and her mouth dropped a little.

Jim looked us over. "Shit! This is getting out of hand. Kill the guy first. But what do we have here?" He grabbed for Cheryl's necklace. "Hey, we got ourselves a Christ killer."

I felt myself tense. If only these mugs hadn't found my gun. They were also three times bigger than me. Now we were going to die along with Grandma Kate and June.

Jim snatched the Star of David off Cheryl's neck with a jerk.

"You're a pretty little Jew girl, aren't you?" he said as he touched her hair. But then he slapped her, and at this, something in me snapped and I just lost it. I lunged for him, knocking him to the ground, and started pounding his face. The other men must have been taken by surprise, because I was able to get up quickly and grab my gun out of the guy's hand. Cheryl took this opportunity to kick the third guy, being a trained black belt. She knocked him out cold, and grabbing the knife, she went over to cut the ropes off Grandma Kate as I held the men at gunpoint. The one called Joe still had his knife and staggered toward me with it. I fired my gun and hit him squarely in the chest. He fell to the ground.

Cheryl went over to the Ford to check on June. Grandma Kate followed her, saying, "Jim said he killed her." At this Kate finally broke down.

Cheryl answered, "No Kate . . . I mean Katherine. She's still breathing. But we have to get her to a hospital."

"Thanks be to God," Kate said, crossing herself. "But I've lost my car."

"We left ours about five hundred yards back," I chipped in. "We'll tie these guys up and call the police once we get June taken care of." I reached down and picked up Cheryl's necklace, which was lying on the ground.

As Cheryl ran for the car, Grandma Kate came over to me. "Who are you really, Kevin?"

"I've told you the truth," I answered. "I'm your grandson from a future time. I wasn't lying to you. I came here to save you. These men would have killed you both. I don't know how it works, but you came to me in a dream and told me to follow you, to save you. Cheryl and I have followed Route 66 all the way from Chicago and came to your time somehow during a Texas thunderstorm."

"I remember that storm. Kevin, I believe you." She then kissed me on the cheek, and I saw such love in those soul-piercing blue eyes.

We carefully got June into my car. Grandma Kate sat up front with me, and Cheryl tended to June in the backseat. My young grandmother must have been too distraught to even notice the modern interior of our surroundings. She kept looking back to see how her friend was doing. June regained consciousness and tried to speak.

"Hush now," Cheryl gently told her. "Lie still and try not to talk. Katherine is here and we're taking you to the hospital. You're safe now." Cheryl was holding June's head in her lap and gently smoothing her hair. June reached up with her hands to search her own face. "I have your glasses. I'll take care of them. Now be still and don't worry."

Kate looked over into the backseat. "It's all right, sweetie, my grandson saved us. We'll be at the hospital soon." Cheryl looked up at me and smiled sweetly.

We arrived at the Mohave General Hospital on Beale Street. The small hospital was built in a Spanish architectural style with a ten-arch colonnade across the front. Two nurses came out and called for a stretcher. Kate helped with the administration and the details of the attacks. One of the nurses came over to us to help contact the Arizona police, who arrived within ten minutes. I asked the hospital to hurry and send an ambulance because one of the guys was shot.

Within two hours, it was looking like everything was buttoned up. They apprehended the men we had tied up. The third one was dead on arrival. We were told there had been a rash of attacks on women across the state and probably beyond. They did not find Kate's old Buick though, nor the guy who drove off with it.

As June was in with the doctor, a nurse tended to Kate's cuts. She also had a bruise roughly the size of a Chicago-style sixteen-inch softball on her side.

A man finally came out to talk to us. He introduced himself as Dr. Leonard Smith. "Your friend is going to be fine. Her face is badly bruised and she has a concussion. There is one broken rib. She will have to stay the night so the nurse can make sure she stays awake until the symptoms are gone. There were several cuts on her shoulder and chest also."

"Well, thank God she'll be mended," said Kate. When the doctor left us, we talked for a bit. Kate continued, "They'll be mending her body but what about her sweet mind? She was so interested in that Jim Schuster. I never would have thought it from him when we met back in Oklahoma. Poor dear soul, my poor June, how will she ever trust again?"

Grandma Kate brought us up to date on their adventure and how June was planning on moving to Oklahoma because of the nice men she had met. Our hearts went out to her. We compared stories and marveled at the times our paths intersected, even across time. But eventually a nurse told us politely we had to leave for the night. We went to book ourselves into the Beale Street Hotel. I was forced to reveal a problem at this time.

"Gran . . . ah, Kate, we don't have enough money left to pay for the room. We might have enough for a small dinner, but that's about it."

"Think nothing of it, Kevin, me boy. Whatever money I have, I'll share with you from now on."

We sat and talked for hours over wine and food. I told her about living at the Spaulding Avenue apartment and how my dad, her son, Sean had turned out. How I met Cheryl at age seven and how she lived there, too. How we found the postcards and knew about Wayne. And how Grandpa John . . .

"Grandpa John, Kate--you have to call him."

"I've been trying to telephone him for days," Kate answered. "I will phone him later tonight. I don't know how to thank you two. I saw my own death in that man's eyes. You both are angels sent from God. Kevin, you still go to church, do you not?"

"Yes, Grandma, every Sunday and most holy days," I answered.

"Most?" she asked. "Well, I would suggest you make it each and every Sunday *and* holy days, me boy. And what about you Cheryl, do you follow in the footsteps of my dear friends the Jacobson's of whose apartment you live? They had a great love for G-d."

"I do, Kate," Cheryl answered calmly. "I even study the Hebrew Scriptures, what you call the Old Testament. I'm planning on moving to Israel with David, my fiancé. Well, at least I WILL be engaged, if we ever get back to our own time."

"I see." I watched Grandma Kate looking deeply into Cheryl's eyes.

"I sure hope June will be okay," I said, breaking the uncomfortable silence. "I mean emotionally as well as physically."

"Yes, tis a bitter shame about that Jim," Kate said. "I used to believe I was a good judge of character. Here I almost pushed dear June into that man's arms while thinking another driver, Rocky, was a menace. Rocky tried to save us back in that saloon. I must find him and thank him. June saw that there was good in him all along."

"Yes, but she also saw good in Jim Schuster," Cheryl interjected.

"Tis true, yes, it's a real shame. Now if you will excuse me, I shall return momentarily."

"Are you heading for the ladies' room?" Cheryl asked.

Kate looked slightly mortified that she would ask that in front of a man. "Why, yes, I need to powder my nose. Care to join me, dear?"

"Yeah, I have to go. I think I've been holding it for over an hour."

* * * * *

As soon as they were out of earshot, Kate turned to Cheryl and asked, "Ladies are quite a bit different in the future, aren't they?"

"I suppose we are, but in what way?" Cheryl asked.

"Well, I saw you knock that horrid man out with just one kick. You wear trousers and speak openly about anything in front of anyone."

"I guess that's true," Cheryl answered. "But I do own dresses, just not ones that would look right in 1946. But, Kate, I also admire women from your time period. You have a strength you don't even realize. Take yourself, for instance. While your husband went to war, you worked your butt off in the factory and then came home and took care of a house by yourself."

"Interesting, but that's just what I had to do. I never gave it a second thought," said Kate.

"Well, I did. You have a lot to be proud of."

"Cheryl, how long have you been in love with my grandson, Kevin?"

Silence ensued as Cheryl looked at her with shock. The question took her totally by surprise. "What do you mean? I never said I was in love with Kevin."

"You didn't have to; it's in your eyes, lass. I can see the way you look at him."

Cheryl looked down at the floor. "All right, yes, I've been in love with Kevin since the second grade. But, Kate, he doesn't love me the same way. I mean he loves me as his BFF."

"His what?" Kate asked.

"Oh, it's a term young kids use in my time. It means best friends forever. He loves me as his best friend, I guess, like a sister."

Kate put her hand on Cheryl's shoulder. "I wouldn't be so sure, my dear. Tis not as evident as when I look at you, but I see things in him, too. He had come to save me, but it was when the man harmed *you* that gave him the strength to save us all. Just don't be too quick to write him off."

"All right," Cheryl answered, "I won't put my tilted stamp on him just yet."

* * * * *

The ladies were laughing as they joined me back at the table.

"Kevin," my grandmother looked at me. "I don't mean to pry, but back there in New Mexico you and Cheryl stayed in the same room. Is that appropriate, as you two aren't married?"

"That was the first time, Kate," I answered. "We needed to save money. It's just a godsend that we found a twenty-dollar bill on the road."

"You say you found a twenty-dollar bill?" Kate asked.

"Yep, just lying on the road," I said, happy that the subject was changed.

"And would that have been in Texas, may I ask?"

"As a matter of fact, it was. Why?"

"Oh, no matter," she answered. "Twas indeed a godsend, Kevin, me boy. Now if you will excuse me, I have some telephoning to do."

Chapter 12
Hip to this Timely Tip

Chicago
March 27, 1946

    John had just gotten home from work after having picked Sean up from his parents. He was dead tired as usual and glad that Sean had fallen asleep on the floorboard of his car. He tucked him in his crib and sat down with a bowl of his mother's soup. The telephone rang.
"Hello?"
"Kate, oh my dear Kate, how are you? Where are you?"
"Arizona? I would have thought you'd be at Karen's by now."
"June? You mean June Franklin?"
"Attacked? You stay put. I will borrow money and board an airplane. I can be there by morning."
"Are you sure?"
"God, no! That's awful. I'll kill them."
"Good! I hope they *stay* locked up."
"Who's Kevin? I don't know of a relative named Kevin."
"All right, dear, you explain it to me when you get home."
"When? I can't wait, darling."
"It's fine, dear; don't worry about that old bucket of bolts."
"Yes, I'll phone Karen for you."
"He's fine; he misses his mummy."
"There's no need to apologize. You just come home."
"It's so good to hear your voice."
"I love you too, hon."
"Bye now."
    John hung up the telephone happy for the first time in a week. When Sean woke up, John grabbed him and started dancing around the house with him. Sean squealed and John laughed and laughed.

Kingman
Thursday, March 28, 1946

Kate, Cheryl, and I arrived at the hospital after breakfast. June was sitting up and appeared happy to see us, although there was a dark spirit behind her eyes. "I thought I was dreaming when I saw the two of you last night," she said.

Kate responded, "Kevin and Cheryl saved us. We were in big trouble. I believe their story now. Kevin *is* my grandson from the future. You should see his automobile. I thought I was in an airplane with all the lights on his dashboard."

She *had* noticed, I thought to myself. June smiled but looked confused. Just then, a nurse came in and told us there could be only two visitors per room and a gentleman was here to see her. Cheryl and I went to wait outside.

June grabbed my hand, and looked from me to Cheryl. "Thank you. Thank you so much for saving me and for saving my dear Katherine."

"Rest now," Cheryl said, patting her other hand. We'll see you later." At this, Cheryl and I walked out of the room and headed for the waiting area.

* * * * *

"Katherine," June began, "I don't want to see any man. What man could possibly be out there?" June sounded frantic. "Please stay here with me, won't you? Don't leave me."

Just then, in walked Rocky with a basket of fruit. "Miss Franklin," he said, "I didn't know what to bring you. So it was either a cactus flower or this basket. I hope you like fruit."

Kate smiled to herself and wondered what it was with men and fruit. Kate spoke first, "Mister Rocky, I want to thank you for your attempt in thwarting those men. I see you have a considerably blackened eye."

"I wish I could have done more. By the way, my last name is Turner. But please call me Rocky." Turning to June again, he said, "Do you like fruit, Miss Franklin?"

June thought he acted differently than when she had met him the first two times. "Yes, Rocky, I like fruit. I'm just not in a very good mood right now."

"I understand, Miss Franklin," he said, putting his head down.

"Rocky, call me June. I wanted to say thank you also for trying to warn me about Jim." June continued, her voice turning bitter. "What is the matter with him anyway? Did you know he was a rapist and a murderer?"

"No," Rocky answered quickly, "I didn't know he and his friends were the ones causing such havoc across the states. I just knew that Jim is an alcoholic and changes dramatically when he's drinking. Even his friends are afraid of him. Makes a man want to give up drink for good."

"Well, all men are louses if ya ask me," June retorted. "Most women too . . . um, present company excepted of course, dear Katherine."

"I know, dear," said Kate. "But Mister . . . I mean Rocky did try and save us and warn you about Jim."

"I know. Please excuse me, Rocky; I'm not feeling myself. Thank you for the fruit." June turned her head away.

"Yes, ma'am," said Rocky. "May I leave you my telephone number? I am at my little house in Oklahoma half the time."

"I don't think so. I'm sorry," June answered, never turning back. "Good-bye and thanks again."

Kate walked him to the door. "Rocky, let me have the number. I'll talk to her. What happened to her with Jim has taken whatever trust she had and . . . if you don't mind the expression, flushed it down the toilet. I'm not sure I'd want to take the chance myself with having you call on her. I never want to see her hurt again. So I suggest you quit your drinkin', and if you're not serious about her, hang up the phone rather than string her along. That is, if she ever does telephone you. I'm telling you this, Rocky: any man who hurts this dear one again has got me to deal with and it won't be pretty."

Rocky saw that her voice sounded serious but her eyes sparkled. She took the phone number and kissed him on the cheek.

When Kate went back to the bedside, June grabbed her hand. "The doctor said I can be released tomorrow and I'll be all right for the drive back home. No train, though. Katherine, do you still have your car?"

"Sadly, no, my old reliable is gone, but not to worry. Kevin said *he* would drive us back to Chicago. His modern car is very comfortable. You can lie down in the backseat with me. By the way, you're coming home to John and my place until you're well. Your father and stepmother are getting on. I phoned last night to let them know."

"Katherine, did you talk to John?" June asked.

"Yes," Kate answered.

"And everything is all right between you two?" June's voice showed the first sign of excitement since the attack.

"I believe it will be," Kate answered. "John and I love each other dearly."

"I'm so glad," June said smiling. "I always believed in you two."

"Do you see, there still are good men in this world, and there's one for you, too."

June's smile faded. "I don't know about that. Yes, John is a good man, and so is my dad."

"Well, I think I was wrong about Rocky," Kate answered. "I see that he is a good man also, deep down inside. He just likes his drinkin' and has an eye for the lasses. But sweetie, his eye went to you. He saw something in you. It's the same thing I see. You are a lovely person. You saw that goodness in him, even when I didn't."

June scowled. "Yeah, well, what about Jim?"

"No one can say about a sort like that," Kate answered. "Could be he is like two men. The one we met who bought you the root beer and the one he becomes at the bottom of a whiskey bottle."

"I know all too well about how drinking changes a person," June replied. "That was my mom. I have nice memories of her sober, but then later of the drunken person she became. She would become so mean and cruel. I know she loved me, but it's hard to remember that in those moments. I remember when they came and took her away. She was screaming and fighting, but she kept yelling, 'No, you can't take me away from my little girl, my June; she needs me and I need her.'"

"Do you ever go and visit with her?" Kate asked.

"Yes, about once a month. She just sits and seems withdrawn, but she's pleasant. Oh Katherine, alcohol can be nice, like the way we share a wine, but why does it grab hold of some people the way it does?"

Kate answered. "Some doctors say it's a illness, like cancer or polio. Once it gets into you, it becomes like a disease; the victims can't help it at that point."

"That's what I would like to do," June said with determination. "I would like to spend my life trying to help victims of this disease. I would also like to save as many people as possible from developing it, if that's even possible. Like Rocky for instance, he drinks with his friends and we were told he likes to fight, but it may not be too late for him. You know, I think I *will* call on him when I get back home. Can you help me get his number?"

Kate smiled. "Now you're cookin' with coal, gas, and oil," she said and held up the paper she had clutched in her hand.

Kate then spent some time explaining Kevin and Cheryl to June.

"He does look a little like you," June stated.

"Yes, and I see John in there as well. I wonder what sort of a woman my Sean-o will end up marryin'."

"You'll have plenty of time to ask Kevin about things like that on the drive home," June said.

"Well, June, they are still out in the waiting room. Do you mind if I take my leave for now? You'll be getting out in the morning."

"That will be fine. I'm feeling a bit tired right now. Not sure what sort of pain pills they have me on, but they make me sleepy. Oh, get my purse and use some of my money to take them shopping. Get that girl a proper dress and buy your grandson anything he wants."

"That's a swell idea," Kate said. "I think I'll do just that."

* * * * *

I waited outside, looking up and down Beale Street, as Kate and Cheryl shopped for clothes. Kingman was a mixture of cowboys and folks in suits and dresses. Cheryl was touched but also apprehensive and decided that not really knowing anything about 1946 fashion, she would let Grandma Kate pick out her clothes. I could barely believe my eyes when I saw Cheryl walk out with legs from here to there under her blue pleated dress. It had short sleeves, belt, and square neckline. The way it fit, I saw curves I never noticed on her before. Grandma Kate had also bought her a pair of white, high-heeled, open-toe shoes, which made her walk with extra care. She looked a bit embarrassed when I gave her the wolf whistle.

Grandma Kate smiled and informed me that this was just an ordinary day dress. That if I liked this one, I'll go bananas over the one she bought for evening wear.

But now it was my turn. Grandma Kate scoffed when I mentioned a zoot suit and told me I'd look like a gangster, but she did want me to have a *proper suit* as she called it. I picked out the fedora and thought I looked like old pictures of Grandpa John. Now it seemed Cheryl had all sorts of opinions and mocked me by wolf whistling as we walked out of the shop. We all laughed and enjoyed a break from shopping over lunch, and then it was on to the hairdressers for the ladies and the barber shop for me.

We stopped back at the hospital to thank June and show off our new clothes, which she greatly approved of. Grandma Kate had to remind me to remove my hat indoors. Here we were approximately the same age, yet she still acted like a grandmother would. I had already grown to love her and June so much.

Friday, March 29, 1946

The next day after breakfast, we went to pick up June at the hospital. The nurse wheeled her to my car in a wooden wheelchair and helped her into the backseat alongside Grandma Kate. Then we were back on Route 66 heading east for a change. It would have been nice to see California and Hollywood in this time period, but I was happy the way things worked out. I was feeling such joy being on the old Route again with June and Cheryl and my Grandma Kate, knowing that I would soon see my beloved Chicago and Grandpa John. I was so happy I didn't even realize at first that I was holding Cheryl's hand. I looked at her and she smiled, but it was a strange smile. Grandma Kate and June marveled at how a car could have air conditioning. They were grateful for it on the hot Arizona road.

The trip from Arizona to Oklahoma was, for the most part, uneventful. June found she could walk a little with our help but had to take it slow. There were times she seemed happy and other times she cried or went far away introspectively. I made great time by driving fast and splitting the drive time with Cheryl. One night in Texas, Grandma Kate even got behind the wheel and marveled at how easy the car handled with power steering and brakes. June asked for the radio often, and we spared them any of our modern IPod tunes or CDs.

Finally, we stopped near Oklahoma City for the night. Even to save money, Grandma Kate wouldn't allow Cheryl and me to share a room. But she briefly considered my suggestion of sharing one with me while Cheryl and June bunked together. She decided against it, saying that June might need her.

While June stretched out in bed, the three of us decided to meet at the bar for a nightcap. When I arrived, I joined Grandma Kate and noticed Cheryl at another table talking to some guy--and wouldn't you know it, he was wearing a zoot suit. She was wearing the evening wear that Grandma Kate had bought her. She had on Grandma Kate's red lipstick. My God, she looked beautiful.

"What gives, Kate?" I asked. "What's she doing? Who's that guy?"

"I haven't the slightest idea," Kate answered. "She was talking with him when I arrived."

She looked at me intensely. I knew I was feeling emotions I couldn't explain, and when Grandma Kate looked into my soul that way, I felt vulnerable. "Kevin, is Cheryl free to talk to whomever she wants? Or do you have a commitment with her?"

I stammered, "A commitment, no, but . . ."

"But what?" she asked. "Didn't you tell me in the car that you would date the opposite sex and then come home to each other as friends?"

"Yes, but it seems different now somehow. Something's changed," I said.

"It had to change, Kevin. How long did you think an arrangement like that could last? You aren't children any longer, me boy. Cheryl wants to settle down and have children of her own."

"I know, she told me. Maybe that's what's changed," I said, downing my drink.

"Tis more than that, that's different," Kate said. "The girl is in love with you. Don't you know that?"

"In love--you mean like *IN LOVE?*" I asked.

"Yes, and furthermore, I believe that if you look deeply inside yourself, you'll see that you are in love with her as well. It's time to grow up. Cheryl has, so you can either follow your heart or let her go." She emphasized her words again, holding out her hand toward Cheryl, "*Follow your heart,*" and then back to me, "*or let her go.*"

I still didn't know what I should do in the long run. I had a lot of thinking ahead of me. But I knew what I had to do in that moment. I got up and walked over to her and the zoot-suit dude.

"Excuse me," I started, "but the lady is with me."

He snapped his head toward me and looked annoyed. "Hey, what's the big idea, Mac? If she was with you, she would be sitting over there."

"Yes, Kevin, what *is* the big idea?" Cheryl asked with wide eyes.

I looked her right in those eyes. "I will let you make up your own mind, but I'm telling you that right now, in this time and place, you are my girl and you are with me."

She looked back into my eyes, trying to assess the situation. She must have seen something there that told her I was serious, that this was important. She held out her hand for me to help her out of the chair. She answered the guy while never leaving my gaze.

"I'm sorry, William, but apparently I'm his girl tonight."

"Oh, that's just swell," William mused. "I sit here alone and this Joe gets two dames."

We joined Grandma Kate back at her table, who was smiling slightly to herself. Cheryl looked as confused as I was feeling. "Kev, what's going on?" she asked.

I didn't know how to answer her. "I don't know, I'm sorry, I'm . . ."

Grandma Kate came to my rescue. "Give him a moment, sweetie. Just let it go for now and enjoy the evening. What are you drinkin' there? I'll order us another round."

I was grateful for her intercession but felt embarrassed and foolish. All I knew was that I had butterflies when I looked at Cheryl. I had never experienced that before with any girl.

That night as I lay in bed, I couldn't get Cheryl out of my thoughts. I was wishing she was here with me right now. But I was torn by my feelings. She was my best friend. How could I lie here and think about my best friend this way? How would I deal with our changing life? Should I let her go or should I change the way I related to her?

* * * * *

Cheryl brushed her hair and tried to figure out how she would fix it again in the morning. She was so confused by what had happened that night and a little upset that things were left unanswered. She thought about how there had been so many times over the years that she had shoved her true feelings for Kevin deep down inside in order to be the person he wanted her to be. She knew it wasn't healthy to continue doing that. Now he had made them surface again one hundred percent. She got into bed. "Oy", she sighed, and then as she always did, she started praying the Shema.

Just then, there was a knock on the door. "Who is it?" she called.

"It's me, Kevin."

"What do you want?"

"Can you open the door?"

"I don't know if I should," she answered.

"But I have something to tell you."

"Can you tell me through the door?"

"No," I said.

"Can it wait till morning? Grandma Kate wouldn't like this, I'm in my nightgown."

"Open the door, Cher; it's important."

She opened the door. "Well?"

"I love you," I said.

"No, you don't."

"Cheryl, I am earth-shattering, mind-blowing, head over heels in love with you." She looked me in the eyes to see if I had gone back to the bar and gotten drunk. "Well, I guess that's all I wanted to say. So now you know. Good night, Miss Bachman," I said with mock sophistication.

Now I was really embarrassed and wondered if I had done the right thing. But before I could shut the door, she flung her arms around me and pulled me inside. We kissed for the first time in our lives where it wasn't just a peck. Her lips were unbelievably soft and our kisses felt right, like we were new creations, made just for each other. Years of bottled-up passion flowed through us.

Later that evening, when it was obvious that I wasn't going back to my own room, Cheryl said, "Grandma Kate is going to be so pissed at us."

"Shhhh, let's not tell her," I suggested and kissed her again.

The Road Home
Saturday, March 30, 1946

I woke up the next morning feeling like I had slept in the clouds. Cheryl was in my arms, and it felt right and good. But we still had a long drive ahead of us, so I snuck back in my room and gathered my belongings. I met Grandma Kate and June in the lobby. Grandma Kate whispered to me, "Did you enjoy your altered sleeping arrangements last night, Grandson?" Her voice told me that she did not approve, but her eyes said that part of her was happy just the same. But how the heck did she know?

After a quick breakfast, we were back on the road again. At one point, Cheryl climbed in the backseat with June while Grandma Kate sat up with me. She started asking me all sorts of questions about the future. I told her about my mom, Janet, and how she had met Sean at a high school dance. How they lived full happy lives before moving to Tennessee. Kate loved that Sean stayed a railroad man and that I had also, but she just couldn't grasp the concept when I explained the electronics and onboard computer systems of trains. She also had trouble understanding how now that we had changed the course of history for the Callahan family, it could all work out differently. From her perspective, all this was just the normal string of events. I started to explain how Grandpa John had changed after her disappearance, but I felt Cheryl kick under my seat, which she did several times, reminding me that I shouldn't say too much about the old time line or the future. But I did tell both June and my grandmother that a great arch would be built in St. Louis and suggested they come back when it was completed.

Cheryl told Grandma Kate about how things turned out with her old friends, the Jacobsons. They were so close that they died within three days of each other. Mrs. Jacobson died first, and everyone said at the time that Mr. Jacobson died of a broken heart.

We stopped in Decatur to see June's parents. Her stepmom was a very caring person and showed June a lot of emotion and love. They let Kate use their phone to call John and let him know how close we were. June's father offered to have June stay with them, but we could see that both her parents weren't feeling up to it and June still needed help getting in and out of bed. They served us coffee and Danish. We stayed about an hour, and it seemed that I never let go of Cheryl's small soft hand the whole time.

We could see that June was happy to be with her parents as she told them all about her adventures with new friend, Katherine, and I could be mistaken but I thought I saw a glimmer of sparkle in her sad eyes when she mentioned Rocky. We could also tell that she wasn't ready to quit her adventure just yet. As much as she loved her parents, it was easy to see that she was ready to change her life. It would have driven her crazy to stay here in Decatur while we were off to Chicago. She had been with Grandma Kate since the hospital in Springfield and knew all about her dilemma with Wayne and John. She had to see the story through to the end.

Upon leaving, we took the smaller Route 51 north until we met up with Route 66 again in Bloomingdale. We were all getting excited that we would be in Chicago soon. I couldn't imagine what the great city would be like in 1946.

Chapter 13
Get Your Kicks

Chicago
March 30, 1946

Our excitement built as the lights of the city first came into view. It was about 6:00 p.m. and dusk was upon us.

"When is the last time you were in Chicago, June?" Grandma Kate asked.

"Much too long," June answered. "I do miss the city. I even miss our days at Bruning."

"Ah yes, Bruning," Kate answered. "Seems like a lifetime ago since we worked there together."

June added, "When I left Chicago, it was because I had nobody left here. But seeing it again, oh Katherine, there *were* some good memories living here."

As we got closer, the city was strange to Cheryl and me. Nothing taller than the Palmolive building bordered the skyline. There was no John Hancock or Sears Tower. Even the Prudential Building wasn't built yet. The Sun-Times building, now the site of Trump Tower, was a decade away, and Marina City was roughly two decades from existing. But then there were familiar sights as well. The Wrigley Building and Tribune Tower looked exactly the same. Up Michigan was the famous Water Tower that had stood there from before the Great Fire of 1871 and the Palmolive Building behind it.

We told Grandma Kate and June about how this city would grow even bigger and greater starting in about 1955. We told them all about the Sears Tower, which for a time would be the tallest building in the world.

"Taller than the Empire State Building?" June asked.

"You bet, taller," Cheryl explained. "They went and renamed it Willis Tower, but any true Chicagoan in our time knows it will always be the Sears Tower."

"Kevin, you should take the Leif Ericson," Grandma Kate suggested.

"The WHAT?" Cheryl and I asked in unison.

"The Leif Ericson Drive. You may know it as Field Boulevard?"

She looked at me and I looked back, puzzled.

"Route 41?" June chimed in, "along the lake."

"Oh, Lake Shore Drive," I said and could see Cheryl in the backseat nodding her head in agreement.

The trip along the Drive was beautiful as night engulfed us. The famous S-curve made sharp turns rather than the nice curvy repairs made in the 1980s. It was funny, but I had always pictured the 1940s in black-and-white or sepia tones. But here it was in normal brilliant color. It seemed odd to me. I explained this to Grandma Kate and she understood. She said it would be like that if she were to travel back to the days of the Irish potato famine or the American Civil War.

We exited at Montrose, which was the very street that Bruning was on. But we wouldn't be passing it, because we turned north at Kedzie. It seemed strange not to see the golden dome of my old church and grammar school, Our Lady of Mercy, near this corner. The old neighborhood was so different. Stores lined Kedzie Avenue. There were Jewish butcher shops, delis, bakeries, corner drug stores, and small grocery shops. But being this was Saturday and the Sabbath, most everything was closed. Cheryl reminded me that technically the Sabbath ended at sundown, so many of the shop owners were busy with preparations for the next day. We knew it wouldn't be there, but both Cheryl and I looked to see if the Golden Crust Pizzeria was at the corner of Eastwood. There was a Jewish bakery there instead.

Because our street was a one-way, we made a left at Lawrence and then another left at Spaulding. The street looked exactly the same as in our time, just a bit cleaner with fewer cars and the trees were smaller. There were kids playing outside, even after dark. That just didn't happen in our time. Another thing that never happened was we found parking right in front of the old gray-stone two flat. Looking at it, I felt like I was home. It was the only home I'd ever known. We walked up the same front stairs that I used to throw a ball against in a game my dad taught me called Pinners.

The Jacobsons met us at the door. They both had warm smiles and were genuinely glad to see my grandmother. She introduced the rest of us and their eyes sparkled. Cheryl said something to them in Hebrew and they seemed delighted. Mrs. Jacobson handed her a pot of stew, saying that we all must be hungry. I noticed their accents were even stronger than I remembered. Jews of Russian descent had a distinct accent all their own.

Grandma Kate used her key instead of ringing the buzzer, as she put it, and we walked upstairs, Cheryl and me helping June. There at the top stood my Grandpa John, youthful and full of life. I had never seen him so happy than at this moment when he grabbed Grandma Kate in a bear hug and kissed her all over her head and face. This was such a surrealistic moment for me. I knew Cheryl felt it too as she slipped her fingers into mine and whispered, "He is so handsome, just like you, Kev."

We walked in the apartment and Grandma Kate introduced us by name. I looked around and saw some of Grandpa John's stuff. There were things that we still had, either in my apartment or at the nursing home. Cheryl pointed out the Victrola we had found in the attic. There was actually a chandelier hanging in the front room. In my place, it was just a cover plate that always looked like a boob to my childlike mind.

Grandma Kate ran to see Sean, her sleeping baby.

"Excuse me, John," Cheryl said, still holding the stew. "Can I warm this on the stove?"

"Oh, sure thing, come this way." He led her to the kitchen, and June asked me to help her onto the davenport. I soon realized that she was talking about the couch rather than a town in Iowa.

Grandpa John came back in. "So, Kevin, I understand you are a relative of some sort."

"Well, ah yes," I stuttered, "sort of. But we better wait for Kate to help me explain."

Just then my grandmother came out holding and kissing baby Sean. It was amazing to look at him, knowing he would grow up to be my own father. I stared at him, trying to see my father in this tiny being. John joined them in a family hug.

I felt wonderful. Things had turned out as they were meant to. There would be some who would argue this point, but somehow I knew it was true. My Grandma Kate came to me in a dream and asked me to follow her, to save her and make things right. But I did have to wonder how the future would turn out. This represented a major change in the course and time line of things to come. I looked over at June and could see she was happy for her dear friend. She liked Grandpa John, I could tell.

We all sat down to bowls of chicken stew and were actually able to convince Grandpa John that I was indeed his future grandson, the only son of Sean Callahan.

During supper, we talked trains. I wanted to show him the pocket watch, but it was nowhere to be found. It was as if nature wouldn't allow the paradox of having it exist in the same place at the same time. The beauty of it was that it would be waiting for me to find in the attic in sixty plus years or so.

After supper, Cheryl came over to me, kissed me, and whispered, "Now that we saved Grandma Kate and all, aren't we supposed to leap out of here like Scott Bakula?"

"I guess it doesn't work that way in real life," I whispered back but then returned her kiss.

My Grandma Kate and Cheryl went to do the dishes, and I felt bad not helping as I always did. But when in 1946, do as the . . .

Anyway, I sat for a while talking to my Grandpa John about the railroad as June listened in. He was amazed by my explanation of how the new engines would work. I could see that he was deeply grateful for our help in bringing his beloved Kate back home to him. It was like he somehow knew how his life would have turned out had she never returned. He shook my hand firmly and warmly.

"It's time for bed," Grandma Kate announced. "Kevin, we'll be goin' to Mass in the morning and we'll be goin' early for confession." She looked at me and I knew she was right. "Cheryl, you will be sleeping downstairs in the Jacobsons spare bedroom. June will be sleeping in ours, and Kevin, you will have to sleep on the davenport until we can make further arrangements. Good night all."

"Yes, Grandmother," I said and she smiled. June told me that this was the happiest she had seen Katherine, perhaps ever.

* * * * *

After Kate got Sean to sleep and made herself ready, she was finally able to climb into bed with her husband. She snuggled closely.

"Oh John, me wonderful husband, it feels so good to be home. I feel like we have a new beginning somehow."

"It's good to see you happy again, Kate. You were so sad when you left."

"Please forgive me for leavin'," she continued. "I don't know what came over me. I was so confused. I have to come clean about something."

Kate told John the whole story about Wayne. She made John understand everything she was feeling and how ultimately it was he whom she wanted and needed.

"My love, I will never leave you again for any reason, I solemnly swear."

"Tell me more about the attack," he asked. "Are you all right? They didn't . . ."

"No," she interrupted before he could say the words that would have sent shivers down her spine. "But they would have if it weren't for Kevin and Cheryl. They would have killed us also. I was so scared, John." She hugged him tighter. "I'm a strong woman and I have you, but it's June I really feel sorry for. I don't know if she will ever get over the betrayal. I don't know if she will ever trust again. You don't mind if she stays with us for a wee time, do you?"

"I don't mind," he answered. "But she might have to get used to the noise."

"Noise?" Kate asked. "And what noise would that be, John Callahan?"

"The noise of me smooching on you all night long." He started kissing her shoulders with loud smacking sounds.

"Now, remember, John. We have a child and a grandson in the adjoining rooms as well."

"All right, I'll smooch quieter," he said.

"John, you're my BFF."

"I'm what?" he asked.

"It's something Cheryl taught me from the future. I'll tell you about it one day."

John then softly and quietly kissed her with long tender passion and made love to her the way it was supposed to be.

April 1946

Cheryl and I really enjoyed life in 1946, living with my grandparents. We were in love and everything was new for us. It was like a dream at times. But we knew that money was tight and we would have to find jobs as long as we were still here. We waited until after the Passover on April 16 and Easter the following Sunday before starting to think about finding work and places of our own.

Grandpa John thought he could get me an apprentice job at Union Station. Cheryl searched the papers for something suitable for her experiences. This was a bit of a problem, as there weren't really any lady cops or detectives in 1946. She decided to try for a Girl Friday job downtown in a detective's office, just to get her foot in the door. I went with her to the appointment, and Grandma Kate kissed us both good-bye and wished her luck.

The interview didn't go very well. The people here must have thought we talked strangely, because they certainly sounded strange to us at times. We decided to take a walk to the Wabash Avenue Bridge and stood there looking around and down at the river.

"It's hard to imagine that the Chicago Fire jumped this river," I said to her. "They never thought it would. It burned all the way to Lincoln Park. It's easy to forget just how big and devastating that fire was." As I held Cheryl's hand and stared down into the river, I got the strangest sensation. I felt intense heat and heard the sounds of bells and screaming. It appeared to be dark except for the light of fire all around us. I felt Cheryl squeeze my hand and then all at once we were back in 1946 at high noon.

"Um, did you see that?" she asked.

"No," I teased. "Unless you mean feeling like we were in the Chicago Fire."

"What the heck, dude?" she said.

"I have no idea," I answered. "It was like my vision of Grandma Kate on the bridge in Oklahoma. Cheryl, do you suppose this is our ticket back home?"

"Could be," she answered, "or it's a ticket to some further past time line. Should we take the chance?"

But I felt in my heart that this would work. That together Cheryl and I could concentrate and find our way back to our own time.

"Let's find a pay phone," I said, grabbing her hand again.

"What for?" she asked.

"To call and say good-bye to Grandma Kate," I answered.

I dialed and June answered the phone on the fourth ring. "Hi Kevin, Katherine is tending to Sean."

"June, we wanted to say good-bye. We might have found a way back home. We want you to know that we both love you very much."

"Do you have to go? Can't you stay here with us?" June asked.

"Dear June, you know this isn't our time. We miss our home, even if it is in the same place."

"I know, you're right," she said. "We all have to get on with our lives. But I'll miss you both so much. Please let me say good-bye to Cheryl, and remember that I will always be thankful to both of you. I love you very much."

She said her good-byes to Cheryl, and then Grandma Kate got on the phone. Cheryl explained what we discovered and I heard her say her good-byes and "I love yous" before giving the phone to me.

"So this is it eh, Kevin, me boy?"

"I believe it is," I said. "That is, if it works."

"I have a feeling it will," she answered. "John says in that blue dress I bought Cheryl, all she has to do is get some ruby slippers and click them together. If I'm still alive in the twenty-first century, I will remember even then what you and Cheryl did for us. It will be strange seeing your birth but not really being able to talk to you about any of this."

"Take care of Grandpa John, will you, Kate?" I said.

"On that, me boy, you can rely. I love you."

"I love you too, Grandma." We both had tears in our eyes when I hung up. Cheryl rubbed my back.

"You ready, kiddo?" she asked.

"We will have to drive to where we can see the water from the car. It needs to come with us."

As we walked back to my HHR, we saw a young couple looking at it. This was something we had become used to, but they had a different look about them.

"Kevin," Cheryl started. "Look at what those two people are wearing."

Sure enough, it appeared they were wearing clothes that looked somewhat futuristic, even to us. I looked around to make sure we hadn't made the jump but saw that we were still firmly planted in 1946. When we approached, they were smiling.

The girl hugged Cheryl and then me, but the guy spoke first. "It's nice to see you two again. Look at how young they look, Kat."

Cheryl and I looked at each other and then back to them. "Who are you?" I asked.

"Oh, sorry," the young man answered. "You don't know us yet, but you will. My name is Cyrus and this is Katya."

"Good to know you," said Katya, very much how they would say it back here in the 1940s.

"We wanted to see this time period and maybe meet your grandmother, Katherine Callahan."

"Why?" Cheryl asked.

Cyrus answered. "Because this is where it all began. This is where you discovered the secret."

Katya grabbed Cyrus's hand, "We have to go."

"So soon?" he asked looking at her. "We just got here."

"Yes, Cyrus, we have to go now."

"Okay," Cyrus said. "Kevin and Cheryl, we'll catch up with you later. Much later." And then they disappeared right in front of our eyes.

"What the heck?" Cheryl said. "Who were they? What secret are they talking about?"

"I don't know," I answered, "but let's just go home. I'm sure we'll find out later."

We found a great spot off Wacker Drive near Clark Street and parked the car.

"We have to concentrate, Cher; we have to really want this," I said.

"That's the problem," she answered. "Ever since you and I hooked up, I really don't care where or when I am. I just love being with you. Part of me misses home, of course, and my job, but then I keep thinking, was it 1946 that brought this out in us, that made our love happen? Will it all just disappear once we're back?"

"Cheryl," I started, "hold my hand and continue looking forward, toward the water. No matter what I say, keep looking at the water." We concentrated as the river flowed below us. It was like we became one with the water. "I love you and I always will. I feel since we fell in love in 1946 then it's only appropriate that I ask you this in 1946. Cheryl, will you be my wife?"

Just then the strange yet familiar feeling came over us. There was a buzzing in our ears and a tingling sensation all over. Behind us, cars whizzed by on Wacker Drive. They were twenty-first century cars. "Cheryl, we're back."

"I know," she answered. "Then it's only appropriate that I answer you here and now. Yes, I'll be your wife. I'll live with you and be true to you and have babies with you. We'll raise them to know both our traditions. I love you, Kevin."

"YES!" I yelled, punching the air. "But we better move this car and go home."

"Okay, let's go home now," she said.

"Cheryl?"

"Yes."

"Babies?" I asked. "How many babies?"

"Not many. Twelve perhaps," she answered with a smile.

Chicago
Present Day

The neighborhood seemed dirtier and more rundown than I remembered. Entering the apartment on Spaulding, we weren't sure what we would find. Would we even still live here? Our keys worked and we found Cheryl's apartment just as she left it. I ran upstairs and found that mine was the same as well…messy. It was as if the trip never happened. Cheryl soon followed me up. I sat down puzzled.

"You would think that something would be different, wouldn't you?" I asked. "Did we just return to the original time line?"

"I dunno, Kev. I was wondering why it was so easy to travel back when we wanted to."

"Not sure about that," I answered. "Maybe we were just linked up to the temporal energy of our own time. Nature wanted us back here where we belong. Those two young people we met said that I discovered the secret, if they are talking about the secrets of time travel, I don't really know why it works, I just know that concentration and water have something to do with it. But it seems we could only really do it when the two of us concentrated together. If I discovered something that somehow affected these young people, then I'm going to have to study it."

"You mean *we're* going to have to study it. All I know is, you have powers, Kevin, me boy." Cheryl said, imitating Grandma Kate.

I had six messages on my answering machine when I hit the button. Cheryl went into the kitchen for a pop. The first message was from a guy at church wanting to know if I would volunteer to usher at the Easter Vigil.

"Cheryl, what's the date?" I yelled toward the kitchen.

"Wow," she answered. "I haven't even turned on my phone yet. Let's see. It's Tuesday, April 1st. Oy vey, it's the same day we left our time in Texas and jumped to 1946. This means we still have today and three more days of vacation left. We got a month free."

The next message was from my mom. She was talking on and on about getting together for Easter. I was thinking, Geez Mom, Easter is three weeks away.

I was only half listening but Cheryl told me to play that last part again.

I backed up the message and listen to my mom's words. ". . . just meet at Grandma and Grandpa's place first and go to church together." Cheryl and I looked at each other as the next message played. There from the answering machine came her voice as clear as we had just left it, Irish accent still intact.

"Hello, Kevin, it's your grandma. Your mother is talking about Easter at our place and that's fine. We're going to invite

Lidia again this year. But your Grandpa and I would like to see you and Cheryl sooner. How about coming for dinner? We haven't seen you busy young folks in over a month. Give us a call when you get a chance."

Cheryl and I were so happy, we danced around the apartment.

"We will have to get the updates from her," I said. "Yikes, we don't know anything about how it turned out, like how did we get these apartments?"

"Yeah, or where Grandma Kate and Grandpa John live," she added.

"D'oh! Well, you're the detective--start detecting," I said.

"Better yet,' she answered, "why don't you just call them? The number is right there on your caller ID."

"Good idea. Hey, when we see them, we can announce our engagement. I promise to buy you a ring. Damn, I just remembered I missed your birthday in both time lines."

"Yeah, well, we were a little busy," she said. "I never gave it a thought myself."

"Well, I do have concert tickets for you."

"They Might Be Giants?" she asked excitedly.

"No, the Harry James Orchestra," I teased. "Just kidding, you guessed right."

She threw her arms around me.

We discovered that Grandma Kate and Grandpa John had moved to a condo in Wilmette. Seeing Grandma Kate with silver hair but still as beautiful as ever was an awesome experience. But the big surprise was seeing Grandpa John. He was different from the man we left in the nursing home. He had a sparkle in his eyes that I only saw in 1946, and his sense of humor was intact. We told them how we had just gotten back from seeing them. Grandma Kate told us she had been waiting for the day she could talk to us about it. They brought us up to date about everything. My mom and dad still moved to Tennessee, but Grandpa sold me the house for a dollar. He had fulfilled his dream of becoming an engineer and worked at the job he loved well into his seventies.

She rubbed Grandpa John's knee. "This is the love of me life, even after all these years."

Grandpa John winked, "That's because I still buy her the best fruit."

"Grandma Kate?" Cheryl started. "What happened to June?"

Kate smiled, but it was a sad smile. "Ah, my dear friend, June. She never fully recovered from the attack that night. But she did finally call Rocky, and after a long engagement and many trips to Oklahoma, she ended up marrying him. Her dream of helping alcoholics was never fully realized. She did get Rocky to quit drinking and settle down, but she was frustrated that she couldn't help more alcoholics to quit. She just didn't know that it doesn't always work that way. She got involved with the Methodist ministries and helped out in halfway houses. They became very good friends with a man by the name of Sam Taylor who helped us one night during the trip."

"Sam Taylor . . . we met him," I said. "He helped us. He's the one who told us about June."

"You don't say." Grandma Kate continued, "He is a very nice man and a good friend. Rocky was a good husband, and for the most part, June was able to regain some happiness in her life. Sadly she lost a battle with cancer just last year."

"Oh, that's so sad," said Cheryl. "I had so hoped to see her."

"I don't understand," Grandpa John said. "You've seen her many times over the years. She used to take you for ice cream."

"No, John," Kate corrected. "Don't forget that Kevin and Cheryl can't remember their childhood the same way. Remember how I explained that to you, dear?" Grandpa John shrugged and Grandma continued. "June and I kept in touch and often talked about our journey down Route 66. We both cried when they decommissioned it in the 1980s. One time when she flew here, we drove back for old-time sakes. We also talked about you two a lot. The last time I saw her, she wrote you a letter. I'll get it."

Dear Kevin and Cheryl,

Your grandmother and I have decided that by the time you read this letter, you will only remember me as I was back in 1946. I wanted to tell you both what you mean to me. I came to see you right after you were born, Kevin. It was strange to look at the baby who I knew would grow up to save my life. And you, dear Cheryl, the skinned-knee little girl who moved in next door to my friends' house. I had wondered when you would come into the picture. I just wanted you both to know that I have loved you for the entirety of your whole lives.

God Bless,
Aunt June

I had to wipe away a tear when I finished. I wish I could remember. But as it was, I'd have to hold on to the memory I did have of her. Grandma Kate pulled out some pictures. My favorite was one of all five of us. Cheryl and I looked to be about eighteen with Grandma and Grandpa and June, taken at Navy Pier. Cheryl and I just stared at it until Grandma Kate said that we could have it.

"Oh, I almost forgot," I said. "We have a big announcement to make. Cheryl and I are getting married."

Grandma and Grandpa looked at each other puzzled. "Kevin, we already know that. You announced it a month ago."

"We did? What does it mean, Cher?"

Cheryl looked at me. "I guess it wasn't just 1946 that brought out our love, I guess it means we were meant to be together in any time line."

THE END

The adventures continue with **Katya and Cyrus Time Pilgrims**
published by
Whiskey Creek Press

Credits

Cover and postcard art: Maura Walsh

ChainOfRocksBridge StLouisMO.jpg: This file has been (or is hereby) released into the *public domain* by its author, David Hinkson. This applies worldwide.

David Hinkson grants anyone the right to use this work for any purpose, without any conditions, unless such conditions are required by law.

Made in the USA
San Bernardino, CA
19 June 2014